"This Is Not Pe...

Hunter took another step toward her. To prevent himself from touching her, he kept his hands clenched at his sides. "Whether you like it or not, I'm your boss. And you're costing me money."

"So fire me," she said.

"If I thought it would solve anything, I would. But I'm not about to give up the one degree of control I have."

This time it was Cassie's turn to step toward Hunter. She looked up at him with anger smoldering in her eyes. "I don't care who you are. I'm not afraid of you. You can't control me."

It was a dare, plain and simple. But as he stared into Cassie's cool green eyes, his anger once again gave way to passion. Hunter remembered their night together, how he'd made her sigh with pleasure and burn with desire. How could he forget her?

No, she was wrong. He may not be able to control her mind, but he damn well could control her body.

Dear Reader,

It's Valentine's Day, time for an evening to remember. Perhaps your perfect night consists of candlelight and a special meal, or a walk along a deserted beach in the moonlight, or a wonderful cuddle beside a fire. My fantasy of what the perfect night entails includes 1) a *very* sexy television actor who starred in a recently canceled WB series 2) a dark, quiet corner in an elegant restaurant 3) a conversation that ends with a daring proposition to… Sorry, some things a girl just has to keep a secret! Whatever your evening to remember entails, here's hoping it's unforgettable.

This month in Silhouette Desire, we also offer you *reads* to remember long into the evening. Kathie DeNosky's *A Rare Sensation* is the second title in DYNASTIES: THE ASHTONS, our compelling continuity set in Napa Valley. Dixie Browning continues her fabulous DIVAS WHO DISH miniseries with *Her Man Upstairs*.

We also have the wonderful Emilie Rose whose *Breathless Passion* will leave you…breathless. In *Out of Uniform*, Amy J. Fetzer presents a wonderful military hero you'll be dreaming about. Margaret Allison is back with an alpha male who has *A Single Demand* for this Cinderella heroine. And welcome Heidi Betts to the Desire lineup with her scintillating surrogacy story, *Bought by a Millionaire*.

Here's to a memorable Valentine's Day…however you choose to enjoy it!

Happy reading,

Melissa Jeglinski

Melissa Jeglinski
Senior Editor
Silhouette Books

Please address questions and book requests to:
Silhouette Reader Service
U.S.: 3010 Walden Ave., P.O. Box 1325, Buffalo, NY 14269
Canadian: P.O. Box 609, Fort Erie, Ont. L2A 5X3

A
SINGLE
DEMAND

MARGARET ALLISON

Published by Silhouette Books
America's Publisher of Contemporary Romance

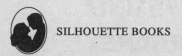 **SILHOUETTE BOOKS**

ISBN 0-373-76637-8

A SINGLE DEMAND

Copyright © 2005 by Cheryl Guttridge Klam

This edition published by arrangement with Harlequin Books S.A.

® and TM are trademarks of Harlequin Books S.A., used under license. Trademarks indicated with ® are registered in the United States Patent and Trademark Office, the Canadian Trade Marks Office and in other countries.

Visit Silhouette Books at www.eHarlequin.com

Printed in U.S.A.

Books by Margaret Allison

Silhouette Desire

At Any Price #1584
Principles and Pleasures #1620
A Single Demand #1637

MARGARET ALLISON

was raised in the suburbs of Detroit, Michigan, and received a B.A. in political science from the University of Michigan. A former marketing executive, she has also worked as a model and actress. The author of several novels, *At Any Price* marked her return to the world of romance after taking some time off to care for her young children. Margaret currently divides her time between her computer, the washing machine and the grocery store. She loves to hear from readers. Please write to her c/o Silhouette Books, 233 Broadway, Suite 1001, New York, NY 10279.

For Melissa Jeglinski, with gratitude

One

Cassie Edwards sank her feet into the sand and sipped her piña colada as she watched the man pouring drinks behind the bar. He reminded her of the prince from Cinderella—tall, almost regal looking, with dark-brown hair, and eyes framed by crinkly laugh lines. He had the physique of an athlete and was wearing a soft linen shirt tucked into a pair of faded jeans.

Although she had not spoken a word to him, she felt a connection, a magnetism that made it difficult to look away. She couldn't help but fantasize what it would be like to be with such a man. How it would feel to touch him. To kiss him. To belong to him.

What had gotten into her?

Cassie glanced around the restaurant. It was situated directly on the beach, an open-air saloon framed in little white lights, complete with a tiki bar and waiters and waitresses wearing Hawaiian shirts. It seemed to be a mecca for romance. Couples were everywhere, holding hands, kissing, cuddling together. It was enough to make even the die-hard cynic a little sentimental.

Cassie felt the sting of loneliness. The Bahamas, she thought, was not the place to mend a broken heart.

But she couldn't think about her ex-fiancé right now. Nor could she allow herself a harmless flirtation. She had not come here in search of love.

She had come to meet with Hunter Axon, one of the most ruthless corporate raiders in the world.

It was a strange assignment for a woman with no business expertise, a woman who was employed as a weaver in an old historical mill.

"Can I bring you another piña colada?"

Cassie glanced up. A tingle ran down her spine as she recognized the bartender she had been admiring. As she stared into his deep, brown eyes, she felt the rest of the world fade away. What was he doing at her table? He wasn't her waiter. Cassie shook her head. "No. No, thank you."

The man hesitated a moment. Then he nodded toward her camera. "Have you taken many pictures?"

He was flirting with her.

Unfortunately, Cassie didn't really know how to flirt. She had never had much of an opportunity. Cassie's and Oliver's families had chosen them for each other ever since they were born two days apart at the same hospital. Growing up, all of the boys back in Shanville, New York, knew she was Oliver Demion's girl. She was off-limits.

Cassie felt a rush of nerves. How did people do this? "No," she mumbled. *What?* "I mean yes."

The man smiled. "Have you been down to the reefs?"

She shook her head. "I haven't had time. I've just taken pictures of the beach. I prefer abstract photos, the kind that capture the essence not the reality. Do you know what I mean? The radiance but not necessarily the, um…" The what? Why was she talking like the nutty professor?

"You're a serious photographer."

She laughed. "No. At least, not anymore. I went to school to study the arts but I dropped out before I graduated." Because my grandma got sick and I had to return home to help her. So I went to work in the mill my fiancé owned and then he dumped me right before he sold the company that everyone in town worked for. Aren't you glad you asked?

Fortunately she kept those details to herself. "It's just a hobby now."

He paused for a moment, looking at her. She felt as if he was studying her, almost undressing her with his eyes. Dear God, he was handsome! She swallowed and shifted her eyes.

"Let me know if there's anything else."

"Right," she said meekly. Was she supposed to say something else? Invite him to sit down? But she couldn't. Or could she?

After all, she reminded herself for the umpteenth time that day, she was not engaged anymore.

But she still felt guilty. And it had nothing to do with her past relationship. It had to do with the reason she had come to this exotic locale in the first place.

She glanced back toward the bartender. How could she have fun when she knew the devastation her friends were about to face? How could she relax when she knew she would have to return to Shanville and disappoint everyone?

How had she ended up in this predicament?

Until a few months ago, she'd thought she'd known exactly who she was and where she was headed. She was engaged to be married. She had a job she loved, a community and town she adored. But life had thrown her a curve ball. In the blink of an eye, everything changed.

In retrospect Cassie should not have been surprised that Oliver broke off their engagement. After all, their relationship had been riddled with problems ever since he took control of the mill. She would've broken off their engagement years ago if she hadn't been afraid of upsetting her fragile grandmother. But it had been her grandmother's wish that she marry Oliver. Her grandmother had claimed that their engagement was the one thing that brightened her days.

It wasn't that she didn't love him. She had grown up with him.

They'd gone to school together and spent their summers working side by side at the mill. But when Oliver took over the helm of the mill, he changed. He became obsessed with money. It became obvious to Cassie that Oliver had big dreams—dreams that did not involve owning a small mill.

In hindsight the writing had been on the wall. Oliver may have talked a good game, but as her grandmother always said, actions speak louder than words. Oliver's actions ultimately proved that he did not want to marry a small-town girl who worked as a weaver in his family's textile mill. And he would never be happy living in Shanville. Oliver was destined to seek love and fortune elsewhere.

But as obvious as Oliver's feelings toward her might have been, Cassie never guessed how deeply he disdained Shanville. She had also never guessed that Shanville would one day be destroyed by one of its own.

But that was exactly what had happened. Oliver had mismanaged the mill so badly he had brought it to the brink of financial ruin. Then, just when she thought things couldn't get worse, he betrayed Shanville and the people who loved him. He announced he was selling the mill—the pillar of their community, the employer of generations of Shanville residents—to Hunter Axon.

Hunter Axon. A corporate raider who had made a fortune taking advantage of others' misfortunes. He was famous for taking over small businesses, firing the workers and closing the factories, moving production overseas.

The sale had caught everyone unaware, even Cassie. How had Oliver arranged this? How had he convinced Hunter Axon to buy a small textile mill that hadn't seen a profit in years?

It took some research, but she finally found her answer. Bodyguard.

Oliver had stumbled upon a patent the mill owned for Bodyguard, a soft, absorbent material. A material, he realized, that would be perfect for athletic wear. And instead of using the patent to turn the mill's fortunes around and make amends, Oliver had gotten greedy.

She had tried to convince Oliver to keep the mill and just sell the patent, but he refused. The mill was as good as sold; the deal done.

So Cassie had no choice but to try to meet with Hunter Axon himself. She was convinced that the mill's fortunes could be turned around if it was allowed to produce the patented fabric.

Cassie had cashed out her meager bank account and flown to the Bahamas to try to talk to him. But her mission hadn't been as simple as it sounded. Hunter's receptionist had refused her an audience with her boss. Desperate, Cassie had even gone to his house, but was once again refused entry. In the two days she'd been in the Bahamas, she had not so much as caught a glimpse of the elusive man.

Now, on the eve of her departure, she was forced to face the truth: she had failed. Demion Mills was doomed to become just another deserted warehouse, its beautiful old looms designated to museums or scrapped for parts.

Cassie picked up her bill. Twenty-four dollars. Twenty more than she should have spent. After all, she only had thirty left, and she needed cab fare for tomorrow morning. She knew she shouldn't have splurged on eight-dollar piña coladas, but she couldn't help herself. She glanced back toward the aquamarine water and set the bill back down. A warm breeze swayed the graceful palm trees that flanked the beach. Perhaps, she thought, she could afford to stay just a few more minutes.

She picked up her empty glass and popped a half-melted ice cube into her mouth. Sinking back down in her chair, she stared at the fiery red sun sinking into the Atlantic.

"Can I buy you a drink?" asked a husky voice.

Cassie almost jumped out of her chair. But it was not her hunky bartender. It was a blond-haired, portly gentleman sporting a sunburn that outlined the shape of sunglasses, making him look like a red raccoon.

"No, thank you," she said. She swallowed the cube. "I was just leaving."

"What's a beautiful girl like you doing all alone?"

"Excuse me?"

"It's a crime, that's what it is. But I have good news. You're not going to be alone any longer." He flashed a thumbs-up sign to some men sitting at the bar. They were snickering and laughing, giving him the thumbs-up back in encouragement.

"If you'll excuse me," she said, "I have to get going."

"Oh, come on," he said. "Let us buy you another drink."

"No, but thank you."

She opened up her wallet, and before she could stop him, he had reached over and pulled out her license. "Miss Edwards of 345 Hickamore Street. Shanville, New York."

"Give that back to me, please."

"You're a long way from home, Miss Edwards."

"I asked for that back." She stood up and glanced around. The music had picked up, and although there were quite a few tables around her, the patrons seemed too busy with each other to notice.

He raised the license above his head. He glanced at his friends at the bar. They snickered and laughed, encouraging him. "For a kiss," he said. Before Cassie could move away, he had grabbed her by the waist. "One kiss."

"Is there a problem?" said a voice from behind.

The man dropped his hands. Cassie turned around and found herself staring into the deep, brown eyes of her bartender.

"No problem," the blond man said.

The bartender's eyes narrowed as he crossed his muscular arms against his chest. He was an intimidating figure with an inherent air of authority.

"The lady here just dropped her license. That's all," the man said, flicking Cassie's license toward the table. His eyes darted nervously toward his friends. They were still at the bar but were staring down at their drinks, pretending not to notice the drama unfolding only feet away.

The bartender's eyes blazed. It was obvious he didn't like being lied to. He took another step toward the man and said in a lethal voice, "I want you out of here now. I prefer to avoid a scene. However," he said, unfolding his arms, "if it's necessary—"

Before he could finish, the man swung a punch. But the bartender was too fast. Like a trained fighter, he spun around and grabbed the man by the lapels, lifting him off the ground. "I'm not going to ask you nicely again."

"Okay," the man said, raising his hands in surrender. "I give."

The bartender set him back down. The man glanced toward the bar. His friends had disappeared. "Some vacation," he mumbled, stumbling away.

Cassie could feel the bartender's eyes on her once again. "Are you all right?" he asked gently.

"Fine," she said. Her camera was sitting on top of the table, its lens cap off. She glanced back at the bartender. Despite her scuffle, all she could think about was his deep, brown eyes. She didn't think she had ever seen eyes so intense.

"You're welcome to use the house phone if you'd like to call someone."

"Call someone?"

"Someone to pick you up. Drive you home."

"No," she said.

"All right, then," he said. "I'll call you a cab."

She remembered the lack of cash. "No, I'm staying close. I'll just walk."

Actually, it was not close at all. After her unsuccessful attempts at meeting with Axon, she had gone back to the motel, a sorry-looking building blocks from the beach. But she couldn't see spending her last night in the Bahamas cooped up in a small, dark room, so she had walked the beach, stopping to photograph anything and everything that caught her fancy: a woman braiding hair, an old man selling shell necklaces, a young child splashing in the waves.

How far away was that hotel, anyway? A half hour? An hour?

She was distracted by a loud holler from down the beach. In the distance she could see her perpetrator. He had rejoined his friends and they were jumping up and down and hollering, making lewd gestures at a group of women.

"I'll see you home," the bartender said. She turned back toward him. He was watching the men. "Where are you staying?"

She hesitated. She suddenly realized she could not tell him where she was staying. Nor did she want him to see her to her hotel. She didn't know him. And although only minutes earlier she had been dreaming about a seduction, the truth of the matter was she was still Cassie Edwards, the town Goody Two-shoes. The twenty-three-year-old virgin. The fiancée of Oliver Demion.

Make that ex-fiancée.

"Thank you for your help, but I'll be fine." No, she could not have him see her home. But there was one thing she desired of him.

He was staring at her, not saying a word.

She picked up her camera. "Would you mind if…" She hesitated.

"If what?"

"If I took your picture?"

He looked at her as if it was the first time anyone had ever asked for such a thing.

"I'll be quick," she said.

"Sure," he said. He stood still, not moving.

She looked through the lens and focused. He stared directly at the camera, looking at her with an intense, yet almost amused expression.

She snapped the photo and smiled. "Great. Thank you."

He shrugged. "No problem."

She wondered if he was just going to stand there until she left. She opened her purse and took out the money. She set it on the table. "Like I said, I'm a photography buff," she began. "Ever since I got my first camera I—"

But she was talking to the wind. He was gone.

She glanced around the bar. There was no sign of him. It was as if he had disappeared into thin air. She sighed. She had a chance and she blew it. What had she been thinking?

With one last glance toward the bar, she turned to leave. Suddenly she stopped. Her bartender was less than fifty feet away. He was leaning against a palm tree, his hands tucked in his pockets as he stared at the water.

She found herself suffering from yet another case of nerves.

Should she hurry by as if she hadn't noticed him? Or should she try and strike up a conversation?

He turned around. He smiled, almost as if he had been waiting for her. "Which way are you headed?" he asked.

There was something about his sweet, crooked smile that made her mind turn to mush and her heart beat faster. "That way," she said, nodding toward her left.

He said, "Me, too. Do you mind if I walk with you a bit?"

She laughed nervously. "Sure."

He stopped. "You do mind, or you don't?"

"I don't mind," she said quickly. He grinned. They began walking again.

She wasn't sure if his being there was a coincidence or not. She almost hoped it wasn't. She stole a peek at him out of the corner of her eye, and when she saw him looking at her, she blushed and glanced away. She realized they did not even know each others' names. But for some reason, it didn't seem to matter. She was content to escape her life and identity, if only for a while.

"Are you in the Bahamas for business or pleasure?" he asked.

"Business," she said.

"What do you do?"

She hesitated. "I'm a…" She paused. She did not want to talk about the mill. Not tonight. Not in this magical, beautiful place. Tonight she was Cinderella at the ball.

He said, "You don't have to tell me if you don't want to."

"I'm in town for a meeting."

"A meeting? Sounds mysterious."

"I assure you it's not." She smiled at him. "So," she said, quickly changing the subject, "I noticed you working the bar. How long have you lived here?"

"About ten years," he said.

"What a nice place to live."

"It can be." He stopped at a small marina and said, "I have to check on a boat. If you're not in a hurry, perhaps you'd like to come with me?"

Once again she found herself hesitating. Part of her would

have liked nothing better than to spend as much time with him as possible, but the other part was telling her she should leave while she still had her wits about her.

He said, "I should admit that I lied to you. I'm not going to let you walk home by yourself. It's not safe for a woman to walk this beach by herself after sunset."

She glanced down the beach. She could hear some male voices. Did they belong to the raccoon man and his friends?

It would be ridiculous to take a chance walking the beach by herself. But then again, wasn't it equally ridiculous to accept a stranger's invitation to his boat?

But was she ready to say goodbye? Besides, as he said, she didn't have much choice. She was not getting rid of him in either case. Not that she wanted to. Not by a long shot. "Thank you," she said.

She followed him down the dock. The boats seemed to increase in size as they walked. He stopped at the last and largest yacht. "There she is."

When he climbed aboard and held out his hand, she accepted his help. She jumped onboard and looked around. "Wow," was all she could say.

It was not only the size that was impressive. The boat looked brand-new. Everything seemed to sparkle with polish—the floors, the doors. It exuded wealth, from the rich mahogany of the hull to the beautiful cushioned deck chairs.

It was the type of boat that looked as if a tuxedoed butler might appear at any moment. The type of boat that was bought and sold with a crew. "Does somebody actually own this thing?"

He nodded and smiled. "Somebody actually does."

"Do you crew on this?"

He hesitated. "When needed."

"I bet that's a nice job."

He laughed. It was the first smile she had seen since they'd left the bar. "It beats sitting at a desk."

"Where is everybody?"

"There's only one crew member that actually lives onboard, and he's visiting his mother in Ohio this week."

"And the owner doesn't live onboard, I take it."

"No," he said. Once again he flashed his crooked smile.

"Mind if I take a look around?" she asked.

"I'll give you the guided tour."

She followed him through a pair of mahogany doors and into a galley. The cabins looked as if they were out of the pages of *Architectural Digest,* each grander than the previous one. At a bedroom door she stopped. She went over to the drapes and felt the material. "Jacquard silk lampas," she said, not realizing she was speaking out loud.

"What?"

"This material is woven by hand," she said. "It's very expensive."

"How do you know that?"

She blushed. How did she know that? Because she spent her days at a loom, making that exact material. "I've photographed it." She ran her hands over the sleek, heavy silk. "It has a wonderful texture."

"You really *are* a serious photographer."

She shook her head. "No. Not anymore."

"Not anymore?"

"When I was growing up, I thought I wanted to be a photographer. I took pictures of everyone and everything."

"Sounds interesting."

She nodded. "I was an arts major in college."

"But?"

"But life intervened. My grandmother got sick."

"And you never went back?"

"No. She needed me. And then when she didn't… Well, things had changed."

"That's too bad."

"No," she said. "I'm happy with my life and the path I've taken. It may not have been the path I thought I would choose, but I have no regrets." She looked at him and smiled. "I don't believe in them, anyway, do you?"

"Regrets?" He shook his head. "Not tonight, at least." He grinned.

Not tonight? She pondered the meaning as she followed him back out the galley and onto the deck. "That's it," he said, turning around to face her.

"No swimming pool?" she teased. "No grand ballroom?"

"I'm afraid not."

She shrugged her shoulders. "I guess it's okay."

His smile faded. For a second she thought she had offended him. He did know she was being sarcastic, right?

"Are you in a hurry?" he asked.

She shook her head.

He nodded toward the lounge chair. "Why don't you have a seat and I'll get us something to drink. What would you like?"

"Are you sure it's all right?"

Once again he smiled. "Yes. Do you like champagne?"

She nodded.

He came back carrying a bottle and two glasses. He opened it up and poured some into a flute. "Cheers," he said, handing it to her.

She took a sip as she leaned back in her chair and breathed in the warm, salty air. "This is nice," she said. "I almost wish I didn't have to go home tomorrow."

"Where's home?"

"New York," she said.

"Is that where your family lives?"

"Lived," she said. "My parents died when I was young. I was raised by my grandparents. My grandfather died about ten years ago and my grandmother…" She hesitated. "A few months ago."

"I'm sorry," he said. There was a tenderness in his eyes that made her feel like crying. "That must be hard for you."

"Yes," she said. She was suddenly tempted to tell him her whole sad story, but she stopped herself. She did not want to tell him about Oliver, nor did she want to tell him about the mill and the horrible Hunter Axon. She wanted to forget about all that, at least for tonight. She stopped talking and focused on drinking.

"You're not married."

She took another sip and said, "I almost was."

"Almost?" he repeated, refilling her glass.

Oh geesh, she just couldn't help herself. Why would she bring up her broken engagement? Didn't she have anything happy to say? Anything fun? "I was engaged but it didn't work out."

"So that's another reason why."

"Why what?"

"Why you looked so sad tonight."

"Tonight?"

"I was watching you."

He had been watching her. Was he…interested in her? "You were watching me?"

He nodded. "You looked like you were ready to cry."

No, he was not interested. He was a nice guy who was feeling sorry for her. Pity was not often a precursor to lust. She shook her head. "I might have been thinking about my grandmother, but I wasn't thinking about *him*—at least, not like that."

"I'm sorry," he said.

"No more 'I'm sorrys,'" she begged. "Please. I'm beginning to feel like a pity case. Anyway, I'm over him. I am. I think everything happens for a reason."

"I agree," he said, nodding. "But it's still never easy saying goodbye to someone you cared about."

She sighed. "True. But sometimes exes can do things that make it a little easier."

"Like?"

"Like leaving you for another woman." Oh damn. There she went again. Couldn't she keep it buttoned up for two seconds?

No. It was not only the alcohol but the anonymity that was getting to her. The ability to talk to someone she would never see again. Someone who did not know her or Oliver, or their situation.

He was staring at her. "He left you for another woman?"

Her name was Willa Forchee. She was about ten years older than Oliver and worked as a vice president for Axon Enterprises. Cassie had met her several times and thought she seemed just as mean and vindictive as her boss was reported to be. In any case, Oliver admitted they had been involved for months. He claimed to be in love for the first time in his life.

Ouch.

But Cassie had not spent much time wallowing in the self-pity of a jilted lover. Every ounce of energy was used up in anger over the mill and herself for not stopping Oliver sooner.

"I'm sorr—" he began.

She put a finger to his lips to silence him. "No more 'I'm sorrys.' Please."

He took her finger away. But he did not let go. He began stroking it. Softly and gently. Even though it was a simple, tender act, it took her breath away. It was far more sensual than a kiss. And so intimate. What was happening? They didn't even know each other.

"What about you?" she asked as casually as she could manage. "Are you married? Have a girlfriend?"

He shook his head. "Neither. I work too much."

His gaze was as soft as a caress. He was still stroking her finger, as if stoking a gently burning fire. She swallowed and said, "You must meet tons of women at the bar. It seemed like the place was really hopping."

"I don't typically date women I meet at the bar."

"Typically?"

"There's an exception to every rule."

He had a mischievous twinkle in his eye. She, apparently, was the exception. It was enough to make her smile inwardly and out. He let go of her finger. "Are you hungry?" he asked. "You didn't eat anything at the bar."

Right. She had spent her dinner money on cocktails. And she didn't regret her decision. Not one bit. After all, she reasoned, a girl had to have priorities. "A little."

"Let's see what's in the kitchen."

She followed him into a large and sparkling galley kitchen. Every appliance was top of the line. "Nice dishwasher," she said.

"Thank you," he said, with mock sincerity. "That's the first time I've heard that."

"My dishwasher just died," she said. "So I'm particularly sensitive right now." Her dishwasher had joined a long list of dead appliances—her toaster oven, her cooktop and her washing machine. She looked around the kitchen. "The people who own this nice dishwasher, where are they?"

He looked at her and hesitated. "Standing in front of you."

"What?"

"I own this boat."

She started laughing. So he was funny, too. Smart and funny. A nice combination. "So you probably cook a lot in this kitchen."

"No," he said. "Usually my chef cooks for me."

She laughed again. When was the last time she had had this much fun? She couldn't remember. It had been a long time since she and Oliver had enjoyed each other's company. But it wasn't always that way. They had grown up the best of friends, enjoying the beautiful town they lived in. In the winter they went ice skating and in the summer they fished and swam in the creek.

Oliver had proposed while they were still in high school and she had accepted. But after Oliver started college, he changed. It was subtle at first. He was no longer satisfied to make a quiet dinner and stay in. Only an expensive restaurant would suffice. And that was not the only change. The boy who had grown up in jeans and a T-shirt began wearing designer clothes and getting manicures. His conversation always returned to money: who had received what job offer with what benefits, who was driving what new car.

Her grandmother had defended him. "He's growing up," she'd said. "Every man goes through it."

But it was more than that, Cassie realized now. They had been growing apart. And the distance had not been entirely due to Oliver.

She still cared about him, of course. She always would. But her love for him was that of a sister toward a brother. She had been more than happy to accept his distance, more than happy to date like a couple from the eighteen hundreds. Social calls that consisted of a glass of iced tea or two in the backyard.

At one point she questioned their youthful decision to marry. But Oliver had been adamant. He persuaded her they were destined to be together, that their decision to marry was still sound.

In retrospect, his were the words of someone who was desperately trying to convince himself. But at the time, she agreed to go ahead with their plans. After all, her grandmother was counting on it. Perhaps, Cassie thought, things between Oliver and her would improve after their marriage. But she was wrong. When Oliver had canceled their engagement, he had done her a favor, however brutal it had been.

"Hey," the bartender said. "Sad again?" And then he touched her.

It was an intimate touch, a hand to her cheek. A lover's touch.

She glanced at him, trying to read his eyes. Still looking at her, he let his fingers trail down her cheek. It had been a long time since a man had touched her like that, and the intimacy was enough to cause her emotions to flood to the surface. No, she thought. She could not cry. Not now.

"He was a fool," he said, obviously assuming she was lamenting the loss of her fiancé. "You deserve better."

"You don't even know me."

"I'm here with you right now," he said. "And that's all that matters." He removed his hand but continued to stare at her tenderly.

How could she be sad when her Prince Charming was standing before her? She only had one night before she turned back into a pumpkin. "So," she said brightly, "what does your chef usually cook in your kitchen?"

He shrugged and opened the fridge. Inside were ready-made bowls of pasta, some delicious-looking London broil and twice-baked potatoes. "Something I can heat up quite easily."

"You're getting into this ownership bit," she said. "Are you sure the owners won't mind if we eat their food?"

When he turned and glanced at her, she added, "I just don't want you to get into trouble."

He leaned forward. "I guarantee it."

"Guarantee you *will* get into trouble or you won't?"

He tucked a wisp of her hair behind her ear. His touch sent another tingle down her spine. "Are we talking about dinner?"

She swallowed.

He smiled and winked, then turned back toward the food and finished heating up the dishes.

When it was ready, he prepared the plates and lined them on his arms like a professional waiter.

"You've obviously had experience," she said, nodding to the way he was carrying the plates.

"Years," he said with a smile.

She grabbed the dinner plates and silverware and followed him to the table, which faced the sea. He lit the candles.

She sat, glancing back to shore. The docks were empty and the beach had emptied out, too. It was as if they were alone in the world. "Where is everyone?"

"It's a private marina."

She took a bite. The food was delicious. She suddenly realized how ravenous she was. She hadn't eaten anything since breakfast. Distracted by the dinner, she didn't even realize her host was barely eating, until she glanced up. He was leaning back in his chair, smiling at her. There was something regal about him, as if he really were a prince.

"I'm sorry," she said.

"For what?"

"My manners. I guess I was hungrier than I thought."

"You have perfect manners." He picked up the champagne and refilled her glass.

"Where are you from originally?" she thought to say.

"I was born in Maryland. But when I was ten my father lost his job and we moved to a little island not too far from here."

"It seems like paradise."

"It can be. But it wasn't quite paradise when I was growing up. It's hard to make a living as a fisherman—especially when you have no experience."

She nodded. "You're an only child?"

"Yes. My mother died when I was young. It was just my dad, my grandmother and me."

"Your grandmother?"

He nodded. "My dad thought I needed a mother figure, so he moved her here from France. She never learned to speak a word of English." He smiled as he remembered her. "I can still hear her now, yelling, *'Ne t'assois pas sur le canapé avec ton maillot de bain mouillé.'*"

"What does that mean?"

"Don't sit on the couch in your wet suit." He smiled at her. He took a sip of his champagne and said, "What about you? Any brothers or sisters?"

She shook her head. "No. I'm an only child, as well." But growing up she had never felt alone. Shanville was a small town filled with quaint Victorian houses, the occasional country store and a small Main Street that seemed to have most everything a person could desire. Nearly everyone who didn't work on Main Street worked for Demion Mills. Cassie still lived in the house where she had grown up, several streets away from Main Street and a short trip through the woods to the mill. She felt as if her co-workers and neighbors were her family. People who had known her since she was born. People who had supported her through the good times and bad. People who, like her, worked at the mill.

They tended the old looms with care and love, producing fabrics that sold for up to $1,000 a yard. They were proud of their work, proud to have covered not one, but three presidential chairs in Demion fabrics. But it wasn't only presidents who had benefited from their expertise. Their fabrics had draped the homes of the rich and famous, the kings and queens around the world. And even, Cassie thought, a millionaire's yacht in the Bahamas.

"Are you done?" he asked quietly.

She suddenly realized she had once again been staring morosely at her plate. He was probably anxious to get rid of her. Cheer up, she commanded herself once again. Stop thinking about the mill. "Yes," she said.

He held out his hand. "Follow me. It's time for dessert."

Two

Cassie accepted his hand, and he pulled her to her feet. But he did not let go. He led her off the boat and back down the dock.

"Where are we going?"

"I want to give you a truly tropical experience." When he reached the end of the dock he said, "Take off your shoes."

"What?"

"Trust me."

She wasn't sure why she needed to take off her shoes, but she kicked them off and followed him onto the beach. He walked over to a palm tree and shook it. "What are you doing?" she asked as a coconut fell to the beach.

He picked it up and said, "I know how much you like piña coladas." He knocked the coconut against the side of the tree, revealing the nut inside. Taking out his tool knife, he used the corkscrew to make a hole in the end and offered it to her. "Take a sip."

She put the brown, hairy shell to her lips and drank some of the sweet, clear liquid.

"Do you like it?"

She nodded and handed the coconut back to him.

"You can finish it if you like."

"No," she said. It was good, but it would taste even better with pineapple juice and rum.

He accepted the coconut and drank the rest of the liquid. Then he cracked it and used his knife to carve out a piece of the meat. "Dessert," he said, holding it to her lips as if he were feeding her candy.

She smiled and bit off a small piece. The whole experience was so sensual that she almost forgot to taste it.

"Well," he said, taking a step toward her. They were so close she could feel his breath on her forehead.

She glanced up at him. "It's wonderful. But why did I take off my shoes?"

He took her hand once again and led her along the water's edge. The warm, sandy water slid in between her toes.

"So you could feel that," he said, nodding toward her toes.

She laughed. She took the coconut out of his hands and held it up to the moonlight.

"What are you doing?" he asked.

"I think this would make a great picture. The coconut blocking out the moon. The light radiating behind it."

"Do you want me to get your camera?"

"No," she replied. For once she did not want to see life from behind the sanctity of her lens.

He set the coconut on the beach, then took her hand and said, "Come on."

"Where are we going?" she asked.

"Absolutely nowhere."

They moved together as one, their arms wrapped around each other. Every now and then they would pass another couple and smile. It was easy to believe, she thought, that they were like them. Husband and wife, honeymooners, lovers.

"My hotel is just up here," she said.

"But your shoes and your camera are back at the dock."

She smiled. "Right."

He stopped walking and she turned back toward him. "Ready to turn around?"

But he didn't answer her. He was staring at her intently, his eyes full of fire. He said, "My God, you're beautiful."

She felt the color rush to her cheeks as she swallowed hard.

He took a step toward her. He towered over her, still staring into her eyes. She couldn't look away. She stood there, hypnotized, completely under his spell.

"May I kiss you?" he asked softly.

She nodded and tilted her head toward him. He leaned forward and brushed his lips against hers. He pulled away and hesitated, as if waiting.

She responded instinctively, reaching her hand around his neck and steering him back toward her lips. He responded with a kiss that took her breath away. His tongue was inside her mouth, exploring the recesses. Deep and sensual, it was unlike any kiss she had ever received.

Only when she thought she might faint from lack of oxygen did he pull away. He stood there for a moment, resting his forehead against hers.

Finally, in a raspy voice, he said, "Let's head back."

He pulled her close to his side, resting his hand on her hip.

It was an intimate gesture, one that intimated ownership. She was his…for the moment. She reciprocated, looping a finger around his belt loop.

What was she doing? She barely knew this man. This…interlude was a fantasy, nothing more. Where could it possibly lead?

But she couldn't think about that right now. She wanted to just close her eyes and enjoy the feeling of a handsome man holding her close, the feeling of being desired.

Before she knew it, they were back at the dock. She sighed, sad that their time together was at an end.

She picked up her shoes. "I need to get my camera before I leave."

"Okay," he said. He almost sounded disappointed as well.

They walked down the dock without touching. He climbed

aboard and once again held out his hand. She accepted it and jumped on. But this time he didn't let go.

She knew it was time to go home. Their night together was over. But before she could speak, he had taken a finger and delicately trailed it around her face. "Don't go back," he breathed, as if desperate for her to stay. Without even questioning her response, she leaned forward and kissed him.

He responded slowly and softly, as if he had been waiting for her an eternity. As if they had kissed a million times before. His hand slid around her waist as he pulled her in closer.

She felt as if the world was spinning away. All that mattered was the energy they alone were creating.

She pulled back and took several deep breaths. Another kiss like that and she would be physically incapable of going anywhere. She needed to leave. Now. "I…I have an early flight. I really should be—"

But she didn't have a chance to finish. He kissed her again, harder this time. All her senses spun to life. She wanted him to touch her, to hold her all night. She wanted to feel his lips on hers for the rest of her life.

Finally he stopped and said, "At least finish your champagne."

She glanced toward the table. The champagne bottle sat in a bucket of half-melted ice. "It seems a shame to waste such good champagne," she said finally. She would have a drink, and that was all. She would go home with her virginity intact.

Smiling, he led her back toward the table. Once she was seated, he dragged his chair closer to her and sat down. He took the champagne out of the ice bucket and refilled their glasses.

They sat in silence, enjoying each other's company. Finally Cassie said, "If this was my boat, I don't think I'd ever leave."

"No?"

"No. I can't imagine a place more beautiful than this."

"Especially tonight," he said. He took her hand and held it. "I'm not often by myself on this boat but when I am, I love to sit out here at night and look at the stars."

She said, "I once tried to photograph the night sky."

"But?"

"I decided some things in life are just too perfect to capture."

He touched her cheek, directing her face back toward him. He kissed her and said, "Stay with me tonight."

She asked the first question that popped into her mind. "Where?" After all, this was not his boat. Was he even allowed to sleep here? She needed all the facts before she made her decision.

"Right here, on the boat. No one else will be here."

It was tempting, but…

"Nothing has to happen," he said, brushing a tendril of hair away from her face. "I'm just…I'm not ready to say goodbye," he said.

Neither was she. "Okay," she heard herself reply.

He picked up her hand and kissed it. "Thank you." Standing up, he offered her his hand.

As she stared at his hand, panic welled up in her throat. She knew that by accepting it, she was embarking on a journey unlike any other.

She glanced at him, hesitating. His eyes glowed with a savage inner fire.

As if hypnotized, she took his hand and he pulled her to her feet. As she followed the bartender toward what she assumed was the ultimate destination, a bedroom, she couldn't help but remember two previous scary moments. As a child, she had once watched a frightening movie her grandmother had forbidden her to see. That night she had lain in her bed, certain that every creak was a ghost with an ax. She had been so terrified she had awakened her grandmother and confessed her sin.

The other time was when Oliver asked her to marry him. She'd had a sudden sick feeling that had taken away her voice, as though a golf ball was being jammed in the back of her throat. Her heart had begun to beat fast and her stomach had tied in knots.

But, she reminded herself, both those times she had recovered. And she hadn't been harmed. Not physically, at least.

Not that she was worried about being harmed. She looked at him once again. He seemed so kind, so gentle.

And she had no doubt he was experienced. He had probably done this a million times before.

Done what? What was she worried about? Hadn't he said that nothing had to happen?

The problem, she realized, was that she *wanted* something to happen.

She swallowed.

No wonder she was terrified. It had nothing to do with him. She was worried about herself. Worried that she might be just a little too anxious to unload herself of the twenty-three-year-old sexual albatross hanging around her neck.

"Hey," he said softly, stopping outside a bedroom. "Are you all right?"

It was now or never. Her last chance to turn back. "Sure."

"Look," he said, brushing the hair away from her eyes. "If you'd prefer that we go back on deck…"

After all, shouldn't she be proud to be a twenty-three-year-old virgin? And in June, on her birthday, she'd be a twenty-four-year-old virgin. Next year she'd be a twenty-five-year-old virgin, then twenty-six, twenty-seven, twenty-eight…. Hallelujah! She might even be eligible for the *Guinness Book of World Records.*

"I want to be with you," she said.

He picked up her hand and kissed it. He led her into a bedroom that had a king-size bed with a velvet coverlet. "Are you sure this is okay?" he asked.

"Yes," she said.

"I just want to lie with you for a while. To feel you next to me."

She smiled, trying to hide her nervousness. They were still standing in the small, narrow hallway. He took a step toward her. She instinctively backed away, up against the wall.

Their eyes locked. For a moment she thought he might kiss her. Instead, he swept her up in his arms. He was strong, stronger than she had guessed. Her heart raced as she leaned back against his chest. She wrapped her arms around his neck, and he placed her gently on the bed. Without removing a stitch of clothing, he slid down next to her and wrapped his arms around her.

He gently massaged her arms as he kissed her. It was a tease, just enough to encourage her to turn toward him for more. He slowly raised her arms above her head. Pinning them down with one hand, he kissed her softly.

They kissed for what seemed like hours, his tongue slipping inside her mouth, probing and exploring ever so gently.

He seemed to be waiting for her silent okay before progressing to the next step. Only when she sighed with desire did he begin to explore her body. He ran his hands over her sundress, slipping his fingers underneath her spaghetti straps. In a practiced move, he pulled down the straps, exposing her bare breasts. His fingers ran over her nipples, followed closely by his tongue.

As he took her in his mouth she felt a warmth spread up from her legs. This was what she had read about. This was what making love was supposed to be.

He reached inside her panties and pulled them off in one smooth motion.

She was no longer thinking with reason. She had gone too far to stop. She needed him inside her.

She pulled at his shirt, clawing him like an animal. Within a second it was off. His pants and shorts followed suit. He was above her, all naked muscle, shining in the moonlight. Once again she was reminded of the powerful fighter she had seen at the bar. But she was not intimidated by his power. She felt safe and protected. Desired.

She took him in her hands and directed him toward her.

It was all the encouragement he needed. With a single thrust, he entered her.

Thick and heavy, he ripped through the last vestige of her virginity. As a searing pain tore through her, she dug her nails into his back and cried out.

He stopped. "I'm sorry," he said as he began to pull out. "I didn't know…."

"Don't stop," she whispered. "Please."

He hesitated, as if unsure what to do. She raised her hips and brought him deeper inside her. She saw him close his eyes, saw the anticipation tighten his face. He was no more capable of stopping now than she was. She moved her hips once again.

He opened his eyes and began to move, gently and slowly. He stared straight at her, his eyes searing into her soul. They were as connected as two people could possibly be.

The pain gave way to pleasure. Intense and primitive, it took control of her body. They moved together, both dependent upon the other. As she moved her body up against him, the momentum built within her, taking control of her mind and body. When release finally came, however, she was not prepared for the intensity. She held on to him for dear life as the dam of sensual pleasure burst, sending her body into spasms of relief. Only then did she feel his body shudder as a slight groan passed his lips.

He kissed her cheek and ran a finger around her lips. "Are you all right?"

She smiled. "Better than all right."

"You're a virgin."

"Not anymore."

He picked up her hand and kissed it, pulling out slowly. "Definitely not anymore." He swallowed. "Had I known...well, I never would have suggested you stay."

"So, I'm glad I didn't tell you."

He smiled, but it was not a happy smile. He looked sad, almost guilty.

"It's okay," she said. "I'm a big girl."

"You were waiting to make love on your wedding night, weren't you?"

She nodded.

He sighed and glanced away. "Did you think this would mend your broken heart?"

"My heart," she said, "is definitely not broken." At least not yet. But she had a feeling things might change tomorrow. He pulled her close and lay there, his arms wrapped around her.

* * *

Cassie awoke to the rocking of the boat. She glanced beside her. He was laying there, his roughly hewn body totally visible on top of the covers. She turned away, embarrassed.

But how could she be embarrassed to look at him when they had been so intimate? Not once, but twice?

She couldn't help but blush as she remembered what had transpired the night before. Making love to him had been everything she had dreamed of. As she looked at him sleeping, she could feel herself melt. His thick hair had fallen over one eye, his arms were spread around the pillow. She would like nothing better than to snuggle up to him and—

He sighed and turned over.

She froze.

She needed to get out of there, before he awoke. After all, what would she say? She could not bear to hear him promise to call and stay in touch. It would ruin everything. Right now it still seemed to be a dream.

And that was exactly the way she wanted it.

She tiptoed out of bed and slipped on her clothes and left without making a sound. She had less than an hour to get to the airport.

Three

Cassie stared at her cold cup of coffee. It was difficult to believe that only a day ago she had been in the Bahamas. Twelve hours earlier she had been making love to a man whose name she did not know.

And now, here she was sitting in a boardroom across from her ex-fiancé. To make matters worse, the cool, impeccably dressed blonde sitting next to him was his girlfriend, Willa, otherwise known as Hunter Axon's henchman.

But if Oliver was bothered by having his ex-fiancée in such close quarters with the woman he had left her for, he didn't show it. He thumbed through a manila envelope and set it back down. "Willa told me what you did."

She perked up. "What are you talking about?"

"Axon's receptionist told Willa about your little trip to the Bahamas."

So that was why he had wanted to see her. When she'd arrived at the mill late this morning, she had been told that Oliver wanted to talk to her the minute she arrived. "It's no secret," she said. "I wanted to see Hunter Axon."

He nodded. "I knew it! You think you're so sly. I know everything that goes on around here."

"Not everything," she said, thinking about her bartender once again. She hadn't told a single soul about her romantic night. It was her secret, one that she would carry to her grave.

"How can you do this to me?" Oliver asked. "You know how important this deal is."

Was he kidding? Was he really narcissistic enough to think she was on a personal vendetta? "This has nothing to do with you, Oliver," she said.

"What, then?"

"This has to do with preserving a way of life, a tradition that has been passed down from generation to generation."

"Oh, please, Cassie. You're talking like a history professor. This is a business. A weak one at that. It hasn't been profitable in years."

She raised an eyebrow as her eyes narrowed. "And whose fault is that?"

But he waved her off, oblivious. "Do you know how lucky I am that I could even sell it? That a company of Axon Enterprises' stature would even be interested?" He was turning red in the face, each word seemingly making him more frustrated.

How could she ever have thought of marrying him? He was not her friend. The man sitting in front of her had become a complete and total stranger. "Well," Cassie said, "you'll be happy to know that I didn't meet with him. I tried, but he wouldn't see me."

"We already know that," Willa said. She reached out a manicured hand and patted Oliver's arm. It was the kind of touch one would bestow on a loyal pet. "Let me speak to Cassie alone." She turned toward Cassie and flashed her a smile that threw daggers. "Privately."

Oliver glanced at Willa. His blue eyes grew large, and he smiled softly, as if melting at the mere sight of his beloved. So, Cassie thought, he really did love her. She knew for a fact that he had never looked at her that way. But she was not jealous. In fact, she had begun to despair of Oliver's humanity and was relieved to learn he was still capable of human emotion.

He nodded and reluctantly walked out, shutting the door behind him.

"Look, Cass," Willa said, in the most patronizing tone Cassie had ever heard.

"Cassie," she corrected her.

"Cassie. I know what's going on with you. I really do."

Cassie looked at her. "What's going on with me?"

"Revenge. Pure and simple."

"Revenge?" Cassie felt as if she'd been slapped. This woman was as bad as Oliver. Did they really believe that Cassie would be so self-centered? Hundreds of jobs and the town's future were dependent on this mill. "This has nothing to do with revenge."

"Well then, what?"

"This town can't afford to lose the mill."

Willa sighed dramatically, as if the conversation was exhausting her. "Cass…Cassie, I want to make a deal with you. I've spoken with Hunter and he's assured me that not everyone will be laid off. I'm in a position to guarantee you a job—but I have a condition."

"And that is?"

"Help us make this transition as smooth as possible."

"What transition?"

"The sale. Hunter Axon is coming here to firm up the deal. I want you to promise you won't…interfere."

Cassie was unmoved. She was not afraid of Willa. She was angry. She suddenly realized why she had been unable to see Hunter Axon. His assistants had been warned by Willa to keep her away from him. "Did you tell your people to prevent me from seeing Mr. Axon?"

"I work for him. It's my job to put out the fires."

"Put out the fires?"

"So to speak." Willa sighed. "Look, Cassie, I'm sorry about Oliver. I really am. But I suggest you take the deal I'm offering you. For if you think I'm tough—well, I guarantee you I'm a sweetheart compared to Mr. Axon."

Willa had offered severance pay of one week for each year of employment. On paper it was a decent amount. But did it make up for the loss of the mill? The mill was the largest employer in Shanville. It supported the town's economy. What kind of job would the people who had spent their lives working as artisans be suited for? And where would they find these jobs? "I'm willing to take my chances."

"You don't know with whom you're dealing. You think Mr. Axon will be inspired by your little sob story? You think he's going to give a damn about you or your little community? He cares about one thing—making money." She smiled. But it was not a kind smile. It was a smile that caused flowers to wilt and water to freeze. She said, "I've known him for years, even before I came to work for him. He is, quite simply, the best in the business. And he does not look kindly on those who stand in the way of his getting what he wants."

"I just want to talk to him."

"If you cause him trouble, bringing this case to the media and what have you, I guarantee he's going to squash you like a bug. Do you understand me?"

Cassie's hand instinctively went to the necklace she had worn since childhood, a gold heart her mother had received as an engagement present from her father. But it was not there to reassure her. Cassie had lost it in the Bahamas.

"I'm not afraid of him."

"Then you're even more of a fool than I suspected."

Cassie glanced away. As much as she hated to admit it, she had a feeling Willa was right. How could she be so foolish as to think she could actually make a difference?

"Let me be clear," Willa said, putting an icy hand on Cassie's. "If you continue to interfere, I'm going to pull the severance package we've offered."

"I don't care about your lousy severance."

"I'm sure you don't. But what about…" She picked up a file from her desk and squinted her eyes as she read, "Luanne Anderson? I believe her daughter has some problems, doesn't she? It would be a shame if she found herself out of work with no severance."

"Are you threatening to punish me by taking away Luanne's severance package?"

"Not just Luanne's." Willa glanced down at the file once again. "But Mabel's…Larry's… Well," she said, putting the list down, "let's just make it a clean sweep, shall we? I mean it's not really fair to give it to some and not others."

"You can't do that," Cassie breathed.

"I can't. But Hunter Axon can."

Cassie swallowed.

"He's done it before, in fact. Several times. He usually gives the workers a choice. They can either be poor losers and get everyone all stirred up, or they can be good sports and concede graciously. Take the money and run, so to speak."

Cassie glanced away.

"In this particular situation I'm going to save Hunter some trouble. If you attempt in any way to contact him when he arrives, I will personally cancel the severance package." Willa smiled once again. She leaned forward and said in a conspiratorial tone, "Oliver told me about some of your recent travails. I've arranged for a severance package that is more than fair. Why don't you take the money and go back to school. Get that arts degree you wanted."

Cassie could feel her cheeks burn. Oliver had clearly spoken about her to this woman. She could just imagine the conversation, just imagine Oliver telling Willa about the simple, small-town girlfriend he was about to dump.

Cassie was tempted to defend her job and her life. But what was the point? Willa would never believe her. To her, Demion Mills was just an old textile factory. As far as Willa was concerned, Cassie should be grateful to her for rescuing her from despair.

"Do we have an understanding?" Willa asked.

"Understanding? This is not about me or you or Oliver. This is about all the people who are losing their only means of support. All the people who have to move away from the only homes they've ever known."

"You're wasting my time," Willa said. "I've offered you a deal."

"Stand by quietly and watch you destroy our town—or try to save it and risk financial ruin for my friends?"

"That's a little dramatic, but basically, yes."

Cassie stood. "Are you finished?"

"Of course." Willa stood and held out her hand. "I admire your spunk, however misdirected it may be. I really hope that your past history with Oliver won't prevent us from being friends."

Cassie left without shaking her hand.

Hunter checked his watch. His plane was late, due to a violent and unexpected thunderstorm. No matter. He was in no rush to reach his destination.

In fact, for once he hated to leave the Bahamas. He hated to think that there was even the slightest chance he was leaving her behind.

"You'll never find her," said the investigator he'd hired. "It's like looking for a needle in a haystack. How can we find a woman with no name?"

But Hunter wouldn't admit it was hopeless. He couldn't. Ever since he had first laid eyes on her he thought of little else.

Hunter felt in his pocket for the only thing that had provided solace in the days since, a heart-shaped necklace.

He had found it on her pillow, its clasp broken. As he clutched it in his hands he felt the conviction surge once again. He would find her. But where? He had searched everywhere. Damn. Why hadn't he gotten her name?

To make matters worse, she didn't know his, either. What if she returned home and had a change of heart? How would she contact him?

He hadn't intended for this to happen. The bar happened to be one of the many properties he owned on the island. He'd stopped in, not for a romantic interlude, but to speak with his employees. But it had been so busy he'd pitched in, helping to tend bar. When he'd seen Cassie sitting by herself, he'd been intrigued. She possessed an almost ethereal beauty with her creamy white skin and deep green eyes. A cloud of long, curly, reddish-brown hair ran down her back. She had the figure of a ballerina, petite with long, slender legs.

But it was not just her beauty that had mesmerized him. She had seemed oblivious to the activity surrounding her. She had stared at the water as if lost in her own sad world.

He didn't usually find himself tongue-tied among women, but when he'd attempted to speak with her, he'd stumbled over his words like a child.

Afterward he realized she'd thought him a bartender, and although he did admit he owned the boat, it had been clear she did not believe him. He had let the mistaken identity slide. After all, he'd thought at the time, what difference did it make? For once it was nice to be with a woman who was not interested in his fortune or his name.

As the evening progressed it became obvious she was lonely, the victim of a broken heart. She needed solace and comfort. He was more than happy to provide it.

But he had misjudged her and the situation. She had not escaped to the Bahamas to lose herself in the arms of another man. She was not looking for a companion with whom to share a bed and some physical comfort.

She was a virgin.

Had he known, he never would have slept with her.

Or would he?

Knowing the pleasure he'd experienced, the incredible connection they had shared, he did not regret a moment. But did she?

Was that why she'd left without saying goodbye?

Had she chosen him out of loneliness? Despair?

It didn't matter. Much to his surprise, he awoke with an overwhelming desire to see her again. When he awoke to find her gone, he was filled with despair. He knew right then and there that he had to find her again.

It had been years since a woman had made such an impression.

He'd been with a lot of women since the demise of his engagement. But he'd kept them all at arm's length. "She permanently scarred you," one woman had said of his ex-fiancée. And until he met his mysterious, auburn-haired stranger, he'd thought she might be right. After all, he had been young and naive when he'd fallen in love with Lisa. She was a fellow college student and together they'd planned their future. When he received an internship at a prestigious New York equity firm, he had asked her to marry him. But shortly afterward he had come home early to find Lisa in bed with another man. To make matters worse, it was his boss at the firm. She married his boss, but not before telling Hunter why. Years later he could still hear her words. *I could never marry a poor man.*

Her rejection had only fueled his desire to become wealthy and powerful. And he had discovered what Lisa had no doubt realized by now, as well. Money did not guarantee happiness.

He glanced back out the window as the plane began its descent. He was surprising himself. He did not consider himself a sentimental type, but he was a man obsessed, consumed by a sweet, brief memory. It had been a long time since he'd enjoyed the simple pleasures in life like a stroll on the beach, a drink from a coconut.

The plane lurched as it touched the ground. He looked out the window. It was snowing in Shanville.

Four

"**A**re you still going to try to talk to Mr. Axon?"

Cassie glanced at her friend, whom she'd known her entire life. She hated to disappoint Frances. Sixty-five years old, Frances Wells—like most of the people in Shanville—lived paycheck to paycheck. If she lost her job at the mill, she would not be able to find employment elsewhere.

Unfortunately, Frances was not alone. The community was aging, and most of the workers were fifty or older. Cassie might be able to move on, but they would not. Still, she couldn't risk losing their severance packages. "I can't gamble with everyone's future. It's a long shot, anyway."

"But it's Oliver. He loves you."

"No," Cassie said quickly. "According to him, he never did. But even if I did have some pull with him, he no longer has any control. He's already given over the reins to Axon Enterprises."

"I don't know how Oliver can stand by and let this happen. If I had known what a devil he would become, I would've swatted his behind while I still had the chance."

"So would I, if I'd thought it would've made any difference."
Frances smiled. "Well, at least I'm happy for you."

"What do you mean?" Cassie asked.

"The severance is just what you need. You'll have the money to move away and return to school." The older woman smiled sadly and patted her hand. "You don't belong in a mill, Cassie. You never did. You belong behind that camera of yours, taking pictures. Working for *National Geographic* or someplace where you can make your dream come true."

"Oh, Frances," Cassie said. Once again, she felt as if she might cry. "I would be more than happy to never take another picture again if it meant you would all be able to keep your jobs." Cassie glanced around her. "And I'm not so sure that's my dream anymore."

"What are you talking about? Ever since you were a little girl you loved that camera."

Cassie shrugged. "All I know is that I can't stand the thought of losing this mill."

Frances glanced at the old stone building in front of them and shrugged. "I guess it was bound to happen sooner or later. We all knew that things haven't been right around here for years. It was foolish to think young Oliver could handle it, just because he had a fancy education."

"I think he could've saved it if he wanted to," Cassie said. "He chose not to." She shook her head. "I wish I'd seen what he was intending. Perhaps I could've talked some sense into him while there was still a chance."

"Nonsense," Frances said. "You know as well as me, Oliver always had a mind of his own." She put an arm around Cassie and squeezed. "At least I can sleep easier knowing that you're going to be okay."

"Okay?" Cassie asked.

"Your grandmother and I never thought Oliver was right for you."

"What?" The news astounded her. "I thought Grandma loved Oliver."

"She loved him like one loves a wayward child. She knew you

two had been friends your entire lives, but she had grave concerns about your future together. 'He makes Cassie happy,' she used to say. 'And that is all that matters.'"

Could this be true? Had there just been a colossal misunderstanding? Had both she and her grandmother tried to convince themselves Oliver was Mr. Right because they'd assumed it to be what the other wanted?

But what did it matter? Her grandmother was gone, and Oliver was engaged to someone else. And she, well, she had moved on, too. With a little help from her Bahamian bartender.

It was days since they were together, but Cassie couldn't stop thinking about him. It was as if he was seared into her consciousness. Everywhere she looked she was reminded of him. Everything she did made her long for him.

It wasn't supposed to be this way.

It was a one-night stand with a stranger. Intimacy without commitment. Lust without love. She didn't even know his name.

So why couldn't she forget about him?

She felt nothing but irritation when she saw her ex-fiancé, but when she looked at the picture she had taken of her bartender on the beach, she felt like crying. She couldn't help but hope that one day she would see him again.

But would he even remember her?

Probably not. His experience with women was obvious. She had little doubt that he had found someone else to share his bed.

She followed Frances into the cafeteria. Employees were packed inside like cattle. At the front of the room were three chairs. Oliver and Willa sat on either side of an empty chair as if waiting for the king. Oliver stood up and said, "Mr. Axon was delayed. But he called a while ago and said he should be here shortly." His face brightened as he nodded behind her. "There he is now."

Cassie turned. There, walking toward her, was none other than her bartender.

Hunter walked through the crowded auditorium, trying not to make eye contact. He had been in this situation many times before. He knew what the questions would be. These people would not be receiving the answers they wanted to hear.

He would be closing the mill within six months. All employees, however, would receive a generous severance package. According to Willa, who had done a thorough study of the area surrounding Shanville, it was more than enough to give them time to find another job.

He looked at Oliver. Oliver jumped to his feet and began applauding.

Applauding? It was overkill, but Oliver couldn't seem to help himself. Oliver reminded Hunter of the rich kid in prep school, the one who was always complimenting the teacher and making fun of the unpopular kids. "Stop please," Hunter said, annoyed. Oliver was kidding himself if he thought these people would welcome him. Willa had said that she had already informed everyone of his intentions.

Oliver's face fell, and he dropped back in his chair. "Sorry, Mr. Axon," Oliver said. "Did you have a nice flight?"

"No," Hunter said. He couldn't help himself. Oliver just annoyed him for some reason. Once again he reminded himself to be civil.

He turned back toward the crowd. "I apologize for the wait. My flight was delayed due to inclement weather. Now, I know you all have a lot of questions. I promise you I will do my best to answer every single one of them." He scanned the crowd. This would not be easy. Most of the workers were older than he had expected. Younger workers typically welcomed the severance package as it was intended, a means to a better way of life. But these people would have a difficult time finding employment elsewhere. "Why don't I begin by telling you a little about my company—"

He stopped. She was standing toward the back of the room, staring at him as if he were a ghost.

She was there.

Run.

Cassie turned and made her way through the crowd, back toward the exit. It was an instinctive reaction, an urge for self-preservation. She hurried as if her very life depended upon it.

Cassie flung open the door and escaped outside. She paused for a moment to catch her breath. She was winded, not from the rush, but from the shock.

She had slept with Hunter Axon.

The realization was enough to give her another surge of energy. She rushed toward the stairwell as her head continued to pound. She had lost her virginity to Public Enemy Number One. The man who was closing the mill and putting her friends out of work.

How could this have happened?

But it had. There was no denying it.

Why had he lied to her? Why had he pretended to be someone he wasn't?

Cassie threw open the stairwell door and began rushing down the steps. She needed to get back to her loom. She needed the comfort of something familiar. A quiet place where she could recover from brain overload.

"Wait!"

The sound of his voice made her stop. But not for long. In a flash she was back on track, moving as fast as she possibly could.

But it was not fast enough. "Wait," he said again, practically jumping down the steps. He grabbed her arm, stopping her. "I've looked everywhere for you."

Looking at him, at the tortured expression on his face, she almost believed him. Almost.

"Hunter Axon?" she said.

He smiled and extended his hand. "Nice to meet you. And you are…?"

As she stared into his brown eyes, her confusion faded. What difference did it make who he was? What mattered was that she had found him again. What mattered was that he had not forgotten her. That he had been looking for her. She took his hand and said, "Cassie Edwards."

"Cassie," he said gently, as if he had been reading the tenderness in her eyes. He held on to her hand firmly, as if he had no intention of letting go. "What are you doing here?"

"I work here," she said, abruptly dropping his hand. She had to forget about their past history. She had to ignore whatever feelings were choking her. This man was not the man she had thought. He was Hunter Axon. And he was destroying the life she had known.

The smile faded from his face. "I don't understand."

"I went to the Bahamas to meet with you."

"What?" he said, the muscles tightening in his jaw. It was obvious that his surprise was genuine. He had not been told of her visit, despite his assistant's assurance to the contrary. "Why?"

"I wanted to talk to you about your intention for the mill. I tried for two days to get in to see you. I went to your office as well as your home."

He hesitated. "So, when you saw me in the bar…?"

"I didn't know who you were. I never would've…" She swallowed.

"A coincidence," he said, taking a step back. It was as if she had thrown a bucket of cold water over his head. All earlier signs of intimacy were gone.

"Yes," she repeated quietly.

The door opened and the sound of high heels echoed through the stairwell. "Hunter? Hunter?" It was Willa.

Immediately Cassie was reminded of Willa's threat. *Let's just make it a clean sweep, shall we? I mean it's not really fair to give it to some and not others.* If Willa saw her talking to Hunter, would she retract the severance packages, as threatened?

It was not something Cassie wanted to find out. "I have to go," she said, turning and heading back down the stairs.

"Cassie!" Willa yelled, stopping her. Willa was peeking over the railing. "Wait!"

Hunter closed his eyes briefly and sighed, as if frustrated by Willa's intrusion.

"What's going on here?" Willa asked, making her way down the stairs.

Hunter replied, "We were just—"

"Mr. Axon was looking for the men's room," Cassie said. She

turned back toward Hunter and said, "And I'm afraid you passed it. It's upstairs, right outside the doors."

Hunter was looking at her strangely.

"Is this true?" Willa asked him.

He glanced at his associate. "How the hell would I know? I've never been in this building before."

Cassie suppressed a smile.

"I'm relieved that you're all right," Willa said to Hunter, flashing a fake smile. "I was concerned when you dashed out of the auditorium in midsentence."

"I was overwhelmed by a sudden urge to…" He glanced at Cassie. "Use the men's room."

"Like I said," Cassie repeated, "upstairs to the left. You can't miss it."

"Thank you." He turned to Willa. "Please give the workers my apologies and explain the situation. I'll be back momentarily."

"Certainly," Willa said.

Hunter ran up the stairs. Cassie heard the swing of the doors. She glanced at Willa and shrugged, then turned and began walking back down the steps.

"I thought you said you didn't meet Hunter when you were in the Bahamas."

Cassie felt her heart jump into her throat. Perhaps their charade was not as convincing as she thought. Cassie swallowed as she met Willa's eyes. "Are you accusing me of lying?"

Willa walked down the steps, approaching Cassie slowly. "It's just a bit confusing. He suddenly bolts out of a conference and I find you huddled together in a stairwell. Quite a coincidence."

"I didn't discuss the mill, if that's what you're worried about."

"Why would I be worried? After all, we have an agreement, right?"

Cassie glanced away.

"It would be dreadful to see so many nice people put out of work, with no money to see them through the long, hot summer."

"Yes," Cassie said. "It would."

Willa hesitated, as if thinking. "Cassie," she said, "I'm glad we had this little talk. I want you to know that I do trust you. And I'm sorry that we've gotten off to such a rough start. I'd like to make it up to you."

Make it up to her? Cassie felt a chill run down her spine. This woman was creepy. She almost radiated evil. "Oliver and I are hosting a little party for Hunter tonight at Oliver's estate."

Estate? Cassie couldn't help but smile. The Demion house sat on top of a hill overlooking all of Shanville. Although it was the closest thing the town had to a mansion, it was hardly an estate. It had been built by a wealthy family in the mid eighteen hundreds. It consisted of twenty-two spacious rooms and ten working fireplaces. Oliver had moved in several years ago, when his parents had officially gone to Florida and given him the reins of his family business. His house was large, Cassie would give him that. But an estate—in Shanville? Hardly.

"Why don't you come."

Cassie looked at her. What was she up to? Was she trying to encourage her to talk to Hunter, just so she could pull the plug on the severance packages?

But could she really do such a horrible thing? And would Hunter allow it...or even encourage it? Or had Willa been bluffing?

Cassie needed to decide whether her hunch about Hunter was right. Would he hear her out? Would he actually listen to what she had to say?

If she was wrong, her friends could lose their severance. But if she was right...maybe they had a chance after all.

"It should be quite the event," Willa continued. "I just got word today that the governor is coming."

The governor? Would he be able to help Demion Mills? It was worth finding out. Willa may have forbidden her from talking to Hunter Axon, but she could not forbid her from talking to the governor.

"Thank you," Cassie said. "I'd love to attend."

"Good," said Willa. "Oh, and, Cassie, it's a formal event so dress is…"

"Formal," said Cassie.

"Exactly," said Willa, flashing her the same, creepy Cheshire Cat grin once again.

Five

Cassie took a step and stopped. It was not too late to turn back.

She glanced up at the Demion "estate." The granite Victorian, never a cheery place, looked almost haunted in the moonlight. Through the windows Cassie could see bits and pieces of the elaborate party inside, a woman's bejeweled wrist and hand, part of a man's tuxedo.

Who were these people?

And why had they come to Shanville?

For an opportunity to meet the great and ruthless Hunter Axon?

It had taken Cassie much of the day to recover from the shock of discovering that the man who had inspired her dreams had also been the one to cause her nightmares.

A coincidence, he had said.

An unbelievable twist of fate. One that could have been avoided by asking the most obvious of questions: What is your name?

That was what she wished had happened, wasn't it? That she had learned of his identity? That the whole evening had been avoided, and that she had returned home with her virginity intact?

No.

As much as she hated to admit it, that was not the case. She did not regret their time together, even though she knew she should.

After all, she had slept with Hunter Axon. So why didn't she regret it?

Because it had been the most perfect night of her entire life.

She sighed deeply. How could this be? How could her tender, sweet lover, the man who had whisked her off her feet both literally and figuratively, be Hunter Axon? Hunter Axon should be a glib, burly man, as grotesque looking and acting as his actions would merit.

He should not look and act like a prince.

But apparently she was not the only one who was susceptible to his charm. Why else would the governor be coming to a party in his honor? One would think the mere sound of Hunter Axon's name would inspire trepidation. After all, his projects typically left a trail of devastation. Joblessness and homelessness were two of the more common side effects.

But as Cassie marched bravely to the door, the governor was not on her mind. All she could think about was Hunter and the fact that within minutes, she would be seeing him once again.

Before ringing the doorbell she paused and glanced down at her dress. Her grandmother had made the material herself, working after hours at the mill. Ruby had sewn the gown. Luanne had added the trimmings. Years ago Cassie had thought it to be the most beautiful dress she had ever seen, and she still felt that way.

Regardless of the dress, Cassie still felt awkward. But why should she? She had been to Oliver's house many times before.

But back then she had come as Oliver's friend. Not as the guest of his girlfriend. She took a deep breath and rang the bell.

Willa answered. "Hello, Cassie." She raised a perfectly shaped eyebrow and gave her a quick nod. "Please come in."

Cassie entered. She winced as she noticed what Willa was wearing. And Willa was not alone. Everyone was dressed in their work attire. The only people dressed for a ball were the tuxedoed waiters.

And Oliver. Although he was wearing casual pants and shirt, he had attempted to make his outfit more festive by tying an ascot around his neck. Cassie couldn't help but think he was taking this owner-of-an-estate thing a little too far. She felt like sending him back to his room to change. But then, her outfit was not much more appropriate.

His eyes opened wide as he saw her. He came marching over, a martini glass in his hand. "Cassie?" He looked at her, confused. "What are you doing here?" She saw him glance at her dress with an expression that was somewhere between curiosity and horror.

"Willa invited me," Cassie said weakly.

"Yes," Willa said. "I was in a jam. Cassie was kind enough to help me out."

"I don't follow," Oliver said, still holding his martini glass. "Why are you wearing your prom dress?"

Cassie stood still. She glanced at her dress, wishing she could close her eyes and transport herself back to her house. Normally she would be in her sweats getting ready to curl up with a good book.

But she did not have to worry about answering. Willa took care of that for her. "One of the servers fell ill. Cassie is going to be taking her place tonight."

Cassie blinked as the words sunk in. It was worse than she thought. Willa had not invited her there as a guest but as a servant. She had walked enthusiastically into a trap.

"Really?" Oliver said, confused. "I thought—"

"You thought what? She's obviously dressed to work." Willa winked at Cassie and said, "You were smart to wear your old clothes, dear. You'll be serving pasta."

Cassie glanced past Oliver, searching the room for Hunter. Was he there? What would he think when he saw her?

But what did she care? It did not matter what she was wearing; what mattered was what she had to say.

No, she thought, she would not allow Willa to interfere with her plans. The governor would be there tonight, and she needed to talk to him. She had a job to do.

"Cassie?" said Willa. "Are you all right? Oh, dear. I do hope there wasn't a miscommunication. You did realize I had asked you here to work."

"Of course," Cassie said quickly. She would not allow Willa, Oliver or Hunter, for that matter, to get the best of her. Though she worked as a weaver and struggled to pay her bills, she was every bit as good as the rest of them. She took off her coat and began to roll up her sleeves. She met Willa's gaze directly. "I'm ready."

"Hello," said a familiar voice behind her. Cassie felt a flutter in her belly. Although she was doing her best to forget him, her body still craved his touch.

"You can start by taking Mr. Axon's coat," Willa said to Cassie before turning her attention to Hunter. "Welcome to Oliver's humble home."

Cassie turned to face him. He was wearing a black designer suit, a bright-blue silk tie and a starched white shirt. It was an outfit that radiated money, power and prestige. His brown hair was slicked back, and his brown eyes were focused on her as if to say, What are you doing here? Willa helped him off with his coat and handed it to Cassie.

"Can I get you something to drink?" Willa asked him.

"Just water for now," he replied, still looking at Cassie.

She had to say something. But what? "Hello, Mr. Axon," she said. "It's nice to see you again."

"And you," he replied, staring at her intently.

No. It was not nice to see him again. It was terrible. Awful. Every time she looked at him she wanted to kiss him.

"You heard Mr. Axon," Willa said to Cassie. "He'll take a glass of water." She handed Cassie her empty glass. "And I'd like some more champagne."

What was going on?

Hunter watched Cassie walk away.

He glanced angrily at Willa. Why was she treating Cassie like a servant?

He was tempted to run after Cassie but he knew better. For

whatever reason, it was clear that Cassie did not want Willa to know about their previous relationship.

"What do you know about that woman?" he asked Willa.

"What woman?" she replied, as if she had no idea whom he was talking about.

"The one who's getting our drinks."

"Cassie? The one you were talking to in the stairwell this morning?"

So, he thought, Willa was suspicious. "Ah," Hunter said. "That's why she looked familiar."

Willa smiled. "I think she works the loom, but I'm not certain."

"The loom?"

"She's a factory worker. She's actually been a bit of a troublemaker, as well. She's threatened to start a rebellion of sorts if we don't acquiesce to her demands."

"Really?"

"I'm afraid so. She even went to the Bahamas to try to meet with you." Willa smiled. "But I took care of it for you. And I've informed her that she's to go through me in the future. You're much too busy to be bothered by details."

Details? Was Cassie a detail?

Hunter felt his blood boil. He did not want Cassie dealt with by Willa or anyone else for that matter. He would take care of her himself. But how could he tell Willa that without making her suspicious? After all, he was usually more than happy to have Willa take care of the personnel matters.

Willa smiled. "That's what you pay me for. To handle problems."

"You seem to have handled her well," he said. He was not liking this, not at all. Willa was an excellent employee, one who had given him years of dedicated service. In her difficult and prestigious position in his company, she was responsible for researching potential properties and companies and determining which ones Axon would attempt to purchase. Many of these were hostile, and Willa had become adept at dealing with difficult employees. Although her methods were sometimes coldhearted and cruel, she was successful. Most of the times he appreciated Willa's skills. But not in this situation. He couldn't help but wonder how Cassie, after threatening to start a rebellion, had fared with Willa's wrath.

Her smile faded. "What do you mean?"

"Well, she's here, isn't she? She must have come to terms with the situation."

"One can only hope," Willa said. Her grip on his arm tightened.

"I wouldn't worry, Willa," he said, searching the room for another glimpse of Cassie. "I can handle myself."

Willa said, "Of course you can." She squeezed his arm again before letting go. "Anyway, we have more important things to think about at the moment." She glanced around. "Like where the governor disappeared to."

Cassie tightened her apron. Her face burned with embarrassment as she thought about the way Willa had ordered her to get Hunter's drink. The woman had succeeded in making her feel uncomfortable, embarrassed her in front of everyone.

But she had not succeeded in distracting Cassie from her mission. If anything, she was more determined than ever to talk to the governor.

Still, she could not help but wonder what Hunter thought when he saw her standing there dressed as if attending a ball. Did he feel sorry for her? Or perhaps instead of pity, he felt something even worse—antipathy. After all, she was certain Willa had wasted little time explaining that she worked the loom in Demion Mills. She had no doubt that Hunter was even more snobby than her ex-fiancé. Hunter Axon, like Oliver, would never be happy with a factory worker.

But what did it matter? She had to forget about Hunter, forget about their night together. For that was all they were destined to have. A memory of a beautiful night.

She walked through the hall, carrying Hunter's and Willa's drinks on a tiny silver tray. Fortunately, Oliver's caterers had a wide selection of aprons. Cassie was able to find one long enough to almost cover her formal attire. But from the guests' reaction she had worried unnecessarily about what she wore. Her apron was a signal that she was part of the catering staff, a servant. In this crowd of snobbish people, that meant one thing: she was all but invisible.

Cassie walked back out to the hall, but Hunter and Willa were no longer there. She peeked in the dining room and stopped. The governor of New York was standing not three feet away, glancing at the lavish spread.

She set the tray down on an antique table and took off her apron. She was determined to act before Willa intervened.

As she made her way toward the governor, she went over the key details of her plea. She would emphasize the importance of the mill to the community, then segue into Hunter's plans to move production overseas. She would ask the governor for his help in preventing the purchase of Demion Mills by Axon Enterprises.

"Excuse me, Governor," she said. "Can I please have a word with you?"

"What?" he asked, turning around to face her. The woman standing next to him stiffened. Cassie suddenly noticed the earpiece in the woman's ear. Like Cassie, she was not a guest. The woman was his security detail.

Would the security woman ask her to leave? It didn't matter. Cassie had bigger problems. Out of the corner of her eye, she could see Willa and Hunter making their way toward her.

"I'm sorry to interrupt, Governor," she said. "But I need to talk to you. I work at Demion Mills. I think you should know that the people of Shanville are not happy about Axon Enterprises buying Demion Mills."

The governor looked startled for a moment, as if surprised by her intrusion. "Well, Miss…" He hesitated.

"Cassie Edwards."

"I'm sorry to hear that, Miss Edwards." His voice, however, was anything but. Bored maybe. Or tired. But not sorry.

He helped himself to a generous portion of roast beef.

"He's going to close the plant," she said.

He shook his head as he speared a tomato with a toothpick. "I was under the impression that he was saving it from bankruptcy."

"That's not true," Cassie said. "All we need is a change in management."

"I'm afraid that's not what I've understood—"

"Please," Cassie said, interrupting him. "Isn't there something you can do to stop this sale? Hunter Axon has the ability to ruin this community. Shanville can't survive the loss of the mill."

But she had already lost his attention. "Hunter," he said with a smile, looking over her shoulder.

She could feel Hunter beside her, standing so close their arms were touching. "This woman," the governor continued, "has some concerns about Demion Mills."

"Really," Hunter said. He glanced down at her. Cassie could see the fire burning behind his icy eyes. So, she thought, he was not happy with her for talking to the governor. Too bad.

"Well," he said, "I'd welcome an opportunity to address them."

To undress them? Her ears were playing tricks on her.

Willa stepped forward and tucked her arm into the governor's as she grabbed his plate. "Axon Enterprises has an excellent community outreach program," she said, steering the governor into the other room and away from Cassie. "Why don't I tell you about it over dinner?"

Cassie watched the governor walk away. That was it. She had lost her chance. To make matters worse, she was quite certain her actions would have unpleasant repercussions. She glanced toward Hunter, readying herself for a fight.

"What are you doing?" he asked quietly.

"I was curious as to whether or not the governor knew about your plans to close down the mill when—and if—you buy the mill."

"And did you satisfy…your curiosity?"

"No," she said.

He gazed at her, studying her carefully. The hardness in his eyes disappeared, replaced by kindness. "You didn't come here tonight to serve food, did you?" he asked, touching her arm.

The feel of his hand was enough to make her quiver. But she

could not allow herself to be distracted. She pulled her arm away. "I came here to talk to the governor. To stop you from buying Demion Mills."

The coldness in his eyes had returned. "Then I have bad news for you."

She stopped.

"I've already bought the mill, Cassie."

Cassie felt winded, as if the news had knocked the last bit of breath from her. "What?"

"I signed the papers this afternoon." He took a step toward her. "I'm your new boss."

"I'm sorry to hear that," she said weakly.

"Why?"

She backed away.

"How can I be happy when a business that has been in operation for generations is being shut down? When hundreds of friends will be losing their jobs?"

"This is not the time for this discussion," he said, eyeing the group of people that was quickly approaching.

When she saw Willa making her way over, she knew she was in for yet another confrontation. And she was in no hurry to cause the loss of her friends' severance. Especially when she wasn't getting anywhere. She looked Hunter straight in the eye and said, "I wish you had told me who you were."

At the mention of the Bahamas, he glanced away. "You left before I had a chance," he said.

"If you knew I was there, if your assistant told you a weaver from the mill had come all the way from Shanville, would you have met with me?"

He paused.

It was all the answer she needed. No. Hunter Axon would never have wasted his time with a mere factory worker. And she had little doubt that he would not have been willing to share his bed with one, either.

"Yes," he said finally.

She glanced away. What was the point? It was hopeless. Hunter

Axon had bought the mill. She was soon to be an out-of-work weaver, an unemployed factory worker, plain and simple. She was not in Hunter Axon's league personally or professionally.

How could she ever have thought that he would listen to her? He couldn't care less about preserving a time-honored tradition or saving the jobs and way of life for hundreds of families. He was interested in one thing: money.

"Hunter?" said Willa. "Is everything all right?"

Cassie did not care to hear Hunter's response. Before he had a chance to answer, she left.

As Cassie pulled into her driveway, she glanced up at the house. The porch light had burned out months ago, and she had not yet changed the bulb. She sighed, making a mental note to add it to the list.

She knew her grandmother would not approve of the way she was keeping house. Her grandmother would've been in the midst of spring cleaning, scrubbing the floors and airing out the carpets. Outside she would've been busy as well, bundling up all the sticks that had fallen during the long, hard winter and stacking them neatly next to the woodpile. She would've raked and tilled her gardens in preparation for her bulbs.

But Cassie had not done any of that. She had meant to, truly, but the last few weeks had been spent in meetings with her co-workers, plotting strategies.

At least, that was her excuse. Although a hard worker, Cassie did not have a natural knack for homemaking.

"You need to pay attention," her grandmother had once said in exasperation. And so Cassie tried. But it didn't seem to help much. When her grandmother would mention that the watering can Cassie left in the backyard was turning rusty, Cassie would grab her camera to photograph it. When her grandmother had mentioned that a mouse had gotten into the cupboards, Cassie stayed awake all night with her camera, ready to snap.

Finally her grandmother had given up. Cassie, it seemed, was forever doomed to make bread that did not rise, sour spaghetti sauce and hard-as-rock cookies. But despite her lack of home-making skills, she knew her grandmother was proud of her.

She had worked hours of overtime to buy Cassie her camera. She'd filled the house with Cassie's photos, hanging them on the wall as if they were great works of art. When Cassie received a scholarship to college, her grandmother had told her that Cassie had made her the happiest woman in the world.

She had been devastated when Cassie dropped out to return home to care for her. "I'm fine," she had protested. "Don't be ridiculous."

But Cassie knew otherwise. The women at the mill had told Cassie of her grandmother's fainting spells and terrible head-aches. They told her that they feared her time was limited.

And so, Cassie returned. This time, however, things were different. Cassie was the caretaker. For nearly two years she took care of her grandmother and the house as well as she could. But she had enjoyed every minute. She had loved her grandmother more than anyone in the world, and her death had left her feeling sad and alone. It was a loss from which she doubted she would ever recover.

Cassie reached back inside the car and pulled out the carton of ice cream she had bought at the convenience store. She planned on handling her sorrows her own special way. The past week called for a pint of chocolate chip ice cream and a spoon.

Out of the corner of her eye she saw a shadow pass under the eaves of the house. She paused. Although Shanville was so safe that most people didn't bother locking their doors, there were exceptions.

Cassie moved back toward her car and put her hand on the handle. "Who is it?" she asked. "Who's there?"

A tall, dark figure stepped into the moonlight. "We need to talk."

Her heart skipped a beat at the sight of Hunter Axon. She felt paralyzed, unable to move.

He stepped closer. "That was the second time you walked out on me."

He was standing in front of her, so close they were almost touching.

She forced herself to shift her eyes, breaking the spell. "What are you doing here?" she asked, making her way toward the house.

He grabbed her back. "Don't walk away, Cassie. You went to a lot of trouble to talk to me. I'm here now. I suggest you take advantage," he said, his eyes hardening.

She paused, looking him over. Would it make any difference? Doubtful. Still, she owed it to her friends to try. But would it help them? Or would it hurt them?

"I would like to talk to you," she said. "But I can't."

"I don't understand. You felt so strongly you traveled all the way to the Bahamas to meet with me."

"That was before…" Her voice drifted off.

"Before our night together?"

"No," she said, meeting his gaze directly. "Before I found out that talking to you could cost everyone their severance pay."

She could see the surprise in his eyes. "What?" he said.

"Willa told me that if I even try and talk to you, she would cancel the severance packages. She said I would never convince you, and we, meaning everyone who works at the mill, would be left with nothing."

He held her gaze. "There are situations where we have been forced to cancel a severance package. But it's not something I enjoy."

Was that supposed to comfort her?

He said, "I give you my word that anything said between us tonight is off the record. I will not hold it against you or the workers of Demion Mills."

He was staring at her intently. His eyes, although cold, were honest.

"Please," he said. "I would like the chance to talk to you."

He had just handed her a pass to get out of jail free. "Okay," she heard herself say finally.

He followed her inside the house. She turned on the light in the hall and said, "I think you know what I'm going to say."

"Is there a place where we can sit down?" he asked.

She straightened. Sit down. Good idea. She nodded toward

the living room. "In there." She moved a pile of newspapers off the couch and made room for him to sit.

She hurried to the kitchen and put her ice cream in the freezer. When she returned, he was looking at a series of photos of a blossoming flower.

"Did you do these?" he asked.

She nodded. "A long time ago."

"And this?" he asked, moving over to the next. It was a picture of a sunflower.

"My grandmother wanted flower photos in this room."

"You're good."

"Thanks."

"Really good. You could be a professional."

"But I'm not," she said curtly. She was not about to give in to flattery. As much as she appreciated the compliment, she didn't trust it. From what she was learning, Hunter Axon was capable of great charm when necessary.

"Your grandmother was not happy about your decision to drop out of school, was she?"

She looked at him.

"I did some research on you today," he said.

Research? He had been curious about her?

"Discreetly, of course," he added.

Of course. Hunter might be a lot of things but she had the feeling he was very discreet when it came to his women. All of his women. Hundreds and hundreds of women...

What was she doing? What did it matter how many women Hunter Axon had slept with?

"Why don't you sit down," she suggested again, motioning toward the couch she had cleared off.

He sat on the edge of the couch and glanced around. "Nice room."

Was he making fun of her? The room was nothing fancy, but Cassie thought it cozy. The furniture was old but comfortable.

"My grandmother decorated it forty years ago and I don't think it's ever been changed."

He was looking at her. She had seen that look before, in the Bahamas. It was a tender look, one normally reserved for sweethearts and lovers. He said, "It must be hard for you, living here without her."

Intellectually, she wasn't sure if he was sincere or not, but emotionally, it didn't seem to matter. She could feel the ice around her heart begin to thaw. "It is," she said.

Get a grip, she warned herself. This was no friendly conversation. She had to stay objective. "But I'm glad that she's not here to witness what you're doing to the community she loved so much."

Hunter glanced away and sighed. "Cassie," he said quietly, "you've made it clear what you think about my intentions for the mill. But you haven't talked about what happened in the Bahamas."

Cassie straightened. Did he really want to talk about that? What was he worried about—that since she knew who he was, she might stalk him or something? Or maybe pretend she was pregnant with his child? "What's to talk about? It was a weird case of mistaken identity. A bizarre twist of fate."

He sighed. "I never meant for any of this to happen. Had I known who you were…" His voice trailed off. But he didn't need to finish. If he had come all the way out here to tell her that he would not have slept with her if he had known that she was not just a factory worker, but *his* factory worker, he had wasted his time.

"Obviously," she said coldly. "If we had known the other's true identity, this would not have happened."

"I didn't say that," he responded. "I said I never intended for this to happen. I didn't say that I had any regrets or that if I had known who you were and why you were in the Bahamas I would have done anything different."

She paused. Now, *that* she was not expecting.

He stepped forward, taking her hand in his. "I've looked everywhere for you. I've had people calling hotels, searching their records."

"Why?"

"Because I wanted to…" He hesitated, glancing down at her hand. "I needed to see you again."

"You…you wanted to see me again?"

"And I found you," he said. "In the last place I expected."

She could feel the world fade away. They were once again back in the Bahamas. He was not Hunter Axon but her prince.

Unfortunately, it was a fantasy. And like all fantasies, the sooner this one came to an end the better. She let go of his hand. "You should go."

He looked at her. Finally he said, "I had hoped that perhaps we might…"

"Might what?" She shook her head. "Even if you weren't buying this company you'd still be Hunter Axon. And I'd still be a factory worker. But because you are Hunter—"

"Why does that change anything?" he interrupted.

"It changes everything. Because of you I'll soon be an unemployed factory worker."

"With the severance, you don't have to be a factory worker anymore. You can go back to school. You can study photography."

"I don't want to go back to school," she said. She shook her head. How could she expect him to understand? "I grew up at the mill, watching my mother and grandmother work."

Her eyes grew distant as she traveled back through time. "I remember looking at the way their fingers seemed to fly over the looms. They worked together, tying the threads and hanging them over the loom. They turned those pieces of thread into masterpieces."

She shook her head as she continued. "There was a time when I wanted to leave. I took up photography and went off to school. But then…" Her voice faded. "I came back." She glanced at Hunter. "And I've never regretted my decision. I love being a part of history, carrying on the family tradition of weaving. I'm not ashamed of what I do. I'm proud of it."

"I'm not saying you shouldn't be proud of the work you do…the work you've done. I'm just saying that perhaps you could look at this a little differently. Perhaps this is not as bad as it may seem. It will give you a chance to reevaluate."

"I don't want to reevaluate. I want to stay here at the mill."

"But the mill can't afford to stay open. I've seen the financials. It has not turned a profit in years."

"It could've. If Oliver had done something with the patent to Bodyguard."

"Not necessarily. I'm not sure the mill could handle the production for that patent. And I know it couldn't handle the marketing. That patent is a gamble. And the mill has no money to put behind it."

Cassie turned away. He had a point. But she was not ready to concede defeat. There had to be some way of saving the mill.

"Cassie," he said quietly, "surely you knew the mill was having financial problems."

She turned back to face him. "The mill was mismanaged. Oliver Demion single-handedly ran a once-profitable institution into the ground. He paid himself an enormous salary and offended some of our biggest clients. He's also never done any marketing or advertising. I know that, under the right management, this mill could be profitable once again."

He shook his head. "I'm sorry, Cassie."

"So that's it," she said. "Your mind is made up. You're going to close Demion Mills?"

"It will be another several months before we will be able to transfer production to our plant overseas, at which point you will all receive a generous severance."

She shook her head and glanced away. "Please go."

He sighed, his vexation obvious. "All right," he said resolutely. "But before I go…" He moved toward her. For a moment she thought he was planning on giving her one last kiss. Instead he reached into his pocket and pulled out her necklace.

"You found it," she said, breathing a sigh of relief. "It was my mother's. I never take it off. The clasp broke a while ago and I jerry-rigged it but—" She stopped. A brand-new clasp sparkled in the light. "You fixed it."

She looked at him and said, "Thank you."

It was a moment of tenderness. She glanced away and fumbled with the necklace, attempting to put it around her neck once more. "Let me help you," he said. Before she could object, he was behind her. His fingers brushed against her neck, causing a tingle that ran down her spine and into her toes. She closed her eyes, her willpower fading. Maybe they still had a chance. Maybe she could still talk some sense into him.

"You can't close this mill," she said, turning to face him.

"What?"

"It's going to kill the town. I don't expect you to care about that, but the people… Almost all of them have worked at the mill their entire lives. It's all they know."

"Which is probably why they've stayed. I'm not cutting them loose without anything. With the mill staying open for a while and the severance package, they will have more than enough to give them time to find another—"

"Even if you're right, and they can find another job, what makes you think they want to?"

Hunter looked at her. She could see his gaze harden. Unfortunately, it only made him look more handsome.

"This is what I do, Cassie. And if it wasn't me, Oliver Demion would sell to someone else. Someone not so generous."

She could feel his gaze sweep over her. He stepped forward and touched her cheek.

She froze. She didn't want to speak any longer. She wanted to touch him. To kiss him.

It was enough to give him one more chance. She took a breath and said, "What about the people who can't find another job?"

"What do you mean?"

"People like Ruby Myers, who's worked for the mill for the last forty years. If the mill closes, how will she make a living?"

He was in front of her. He raised her chin toward him with his index finger. "She will have social security and a handsome severance."

Cassie took a step back, moving away from him. "That's not good enough. Frances Wells can't leave town, either. She's caring for a sick husband. Xavier Scott can't leave, neither can Miranda Peters or Richard Smith."

"Perhaps we can work out a different severance. Perhaps we can give them more money."

"That's very generous of you, but I'm not interested in negotiating a severance."

"What exactly were you suggesting, then?"

She straightened. "Sell us back the mill."

"Are you prepared to make me an offer?"

Cassie glanced away. She had spoken with many banks since she found out Oliver was trying to sell the mill. But none had been willing to finance a loan.

"Cassie," Hunter said, and once again the warmth was gone from his voice. From the cold way in which he regarded her, she thought for a moment she might have gone too far. That perhaps he would renege and cancel the severance package. "I'm not in the business of giving away properties. And I'm not about to finance an operation that has not turned a profit for years."

She nodded. It was hopeless. He would not change his mind. "Goodbye, Mr. Axon."

He sighed. "Just ask yourself this, Cassie. What will you and all your friends do if I sold you the mill and you were forced to declare bankruptcy? Just imagine. No severance package, no last pay period. Just gone."

"We won't have the opportunity to find out, will we?"

He gave her one last glance before turning away. As he walked toward the door, he stopped.

Suddenly Cassie realized what he was looking at. The photo she had taken of Hunter on the beach was sitting on top of the table. She had printed it out as soon as she returned home, a reminder of the mysterious and kind man to whom she had given her heart.

He glanced back at her and looked, for a moment, as if he might speak. Instead he turned back toward the door and left. Cassie ran to the door and leaned outside.

"Hunter," she said, her voice stopping him. "Thank you for returning my heart."

And with that she slammed the door.

Six

Cassie looked at the white posterboard. She picked up a red marker and wrote: Workers on Strike.

"Here you go, Mabel," she said, handing it to the grey-haired woman in front of her. "You can go join the others."

It was a cold, drizzly day, typical of early spring. The winds whipped in from the mountains, swirling around town and chilling even the sturdiest of souls. But no one noticed the biting rain or the invincible wind. They had more important things on their minds. Like the strike.

After Hunter had left, Cassie had called everyone and anyone she could think of. Her message was the same: Hunter Axon would not listen. Urgent action was needed.

But what?

Christine Humblegot, who worked as Oliver's secretary, said she had overheard Willa tell Oliver that because the plant in China would not be up and running for another three months, she was counting on the workers at Demion Mills to begin producing Bodyguard samples so that they could deliver on time.

In other words, Hunter needed them. At least temporarily.

It was their only bargaining chip.

A strike might make him more willing to negotiate. Of course, a man like Hunter would be able to find a way to work around the strike—but it would cause him some headaches.

"This is so exciting," Mabel said. "I've never done anything like this in all my sixty-three years." Mabel held the poster proudly above her head and stopped. "Do you think the police will arrest us?"

"I doubt it," Cassie said. "Herb has his hands full." Cassie nodded toward Herb Blansfield, Shanville's sheriff. He was standing by the entrance to the mill, waving a sign that said Keep Jobs In Shanville. Although it had been years since he last worked in the mill, his wife and daughter were employed as weavers.

Cassie smiled as she looked over the crowd. She had explained the risks to each and every one of them. But that seemed to only firm their resolve. Despite the risk, every single member of the mill had enthusiastically joined the strike. They were courageous and determined. No one was willing to see the mill disappear into the hands of a company who had only one intention: to destroy it.

So the whole community had turned out to show its resolve. Luanne was there with her six daughters, all mill employees. Christine was there with her grandparents.

If Hunter Axon thought they would just roll over and hand him the keys to their beloved mill, he was wrong.

Hunter left Cassie's with one agenda: he wanted to kiss her.

Not that a simple kiss would quench his thirst. His need for her had taken on a life of its own, growing stronger by the day. The thought of never seeing her again had brought him to the brink of despair.

To have found her was a miracle.

But their reunion had fallen quite short of his anticipation. Instead of falling into his arms, she had been ready to run him out of town on a rail.

Once again he found himself thinking about what had transpired the previous evening. Instead of making love they'd argued about Cassie's desire to save a broken-down mill.

How could she expect him to fund a business that had not shown a profit for years, a business that was on the verge of bankruptcy?

Yet Cassie's reaction was not unique. In his years of business he had encountered many workers who, like Cassie, made him desperate offers to save their businesses. He had been vilified as a devil, an unfeeling corporate raider who took advantage of other people's misfortune.

Some of them had given him pause. A few had made him wonder if he had done the right thing.

But of course he had. After all, he did not buy successful businesses. Their misfortune was brought on by the same reasons that were responsible for the demise of Demion Mills—a greedy heir who had no business expertise and workers who were paid more than the company could afford. Sometimes the product needed to be redefined; sometimes the whole concept of the business needed to be simplified.

He would figure out the solution and roll the company into Axon Enterprises where it would become part of a profitable, money-making organization.

It was the only way. And, most of the time at least, the workers eventually realized that they had no choice but to accept their fate.

Sooner or later Cassie would realize that, too. In the meantime he needed to win her back. He needed to make her forget about the mill.

But how? She had made it clear the night before where she stood. She was not interested in him unless he reconsidered his plans for the mill.

But that was not an option.

He needed to persuade her that his buying the mill was the best scenario in a long list of awful ones. And then they would pick up where they left off in the Bahamas. Once again he remembered how she felt next to him, her warm silky body resting beside him.

Flowers, he thought. He would start with flowers. A dozen roses each day and—

As he pulled into the parking lot he was suddenly distracted by the people waving signs in front of the mill. He stepped out of his car and discovered Willa and Oliver standing side by side, looking at the strikers.

"I can't believe it," he heard Oliver say.

"What's going on?" asked Hunter.

"They're striking," said Willa.

"What do we care?" Oliver said. "We're moving the operations to China, anyway." He smiled at Willa. But she did not smile back.

"We do care," she said. "We need to keep this mill operational until China is set up and ready to go."

"So," Oliver said, the smile fading from his lips, "what do we do?"

Hunter glanced at Willa. "Find out who the organizer is."

"And?"

"Bring them to me," he said in a voice that inspired fear in even the strongest of men. With that he brushed past Oliver and headed toward the mill.

If these people thought he could be taken down by a simple strike, they were mistaken. If they wanted a fight, they were going to get it. He was done being Mr. Nice Guy.

Cassie sipped her steaming hot chocolate. She had seen Hunter from a distance, and the unhappy look on his face was enough to bring a smile to her lips. He was learning that the artisans at the mill were a bit tougher and more well organized than he thought.

"Look who's coming," Ruby said, motioning behind Cassie. Cassie turned around. Willa was walking toward her, her lips taut in a half smirk, half smile. As she walked, the crowd became silent and parted, staring as she passed. She did not acknowledge them but kept her eyes focused on Cassie.

Cassie stood up straight and inhaled, as if bracing for a fight.

Willa stopped in front of her. "Cassie," she said, "can I talk to you for a minute?"

Cassie nodded. She handed the remainder of her hot chocolate to Ruby, who accepted it with a comforting nod. Then Cassie turned and followed Willa back into the empty building. They
walked in silence to the cafeteria. Once inside the cavernous
room, Willa turned to face her. She said, "I believe you owe me
an apology."

"We had no choice but to strike," Cassie explained. "I tried
to speak with you—"

"I'm not talking about the strike," Willa said in a tone so
sweet it was bitter. "I was talking about last night."

Cassie suddenly remembered that she had left the party
shortly after her confrontation with Hunter.

"Honestly, Cassie," Willa said, hands on her hips. "I have a
mind to fire you right now. How dare you harass the governor."

Cassie did not look away. She was not afraid of Willa, nor was
she intimidated by her threats.

Willa raised an eyebrow. "Don't make the mistake of thinking that your…relationship with Hunter will protect you."

Cassie swallowed. Had Hunter confided in Willa? "I don't
have a relationship with Mr. Axon." And she wasn't lying. A one-
night stand hardly qualified as a relationship.

"You're a fool," Willa said. "Whatever it is you're doing to
him or with him, it's not going to make any difference in the long
run. Do you understand me?"

"No," Cassie said. "I don't."

"Hunter Axon is a kiss-and-don't-call type of guy. He may be
intrigued by you, but it'll fade as soon as you start interfering
with business. If you're interested in landing more than a job, I'd
suggest you stop interfering with Hunter's plans."

"You're wrong about my interest in Hunter. I want to save this
mill. I'll do whatever I can to make that happen."

"Even if it means giving Hunter your virginity?"

"What?" Cassie said, startled. How could she know about
that? How could Hunter have confided such an intimate detail?

"Don't think Oliver didn't tell me about how you've held on
to it for all these long years."

Oliver. Oliver had told her she was a virgin. Hunter had kept his silence.

"Is that what you've offered Hunter?" Willa asked. "A night with a virgin?"

"I've had enough," Cassie said. She turned to leave.

But Willa stopped her with her words. "Do your friends know of your feelings for the man who's destroying their company?"

"I told you, Willa, you're wrong." Once again Cassie reminded herself that the man who had captured her heart was fictitious, a figment of her imagination. He bore no resemblance to the man known as Hunter Axon.

Willa looked her over carefully. "Perhaps," she said. "But I doubt it. I'm never wrong."

Cassie glanced away. She wanted to say something, but what?

"He'll never care about you," Willa said. "Other women have tried, just like you, to get his attention. They only succeeded in irritating him. Hunter does not like to be distracted from his mission."

Once again Cassie faced Willa. "And what is that?"

Willa smiled. "Making money, of course."

Hunter had made a decision. He would cancel one week of severance for every hour of the strike. A person who had worked there for eight years would erase his entire severance in one day.

It was a drastic measure, but necessary. He had little patience for games.

Willa entered without knocking and crossed her arms.

Hunter snapped his phone shut. "What are their demands?" he asked, rolling up his sleeves as if readying for a fight.

Willa smiled smugly. "I've found the organizer. I think she should tell you herself." With a dramatic sweep of her arm, Willa stepped aside.

Cassie.

She stood still, her arms crossed in front of her and her eyes defiant. A bandanna was tied around her head, holding back her beautiful reddish-brown hair. She was wearing a loose-fitting flannel shirt rolled up at the sleeves and an old pair of jeans.

As far as Hunter was concerned, he had never been presented with a more worthy foe. Nor had he ever seen anyone so beautiful.

"You?" he heard himself say.

Willa said, "She's the one behind this ridiculous strike. She was working the phones all night, organizing the workers. According to Oliver, they've never done anything like this before."

He continued to look at Cassie. "Why?"

Cassie stood up straight and said, "We're not going to let you take this mill away from us. Not without a fight."

"I didn't take this mill away from you," he said. "The Demions did."

"You are the owner," she said, narrowing her fiery green eyes. "Correct?"

As he stared at the woman in front of him, he could feel his resolve melt. How could he tell her that he was canceling her severance? How could he hurt her?

He had to admit he admired her spirit. But what could she possibly hope to gain by such a ruse? The mill would be closing in a few months. He could bring in other workers in the meantime. Or could he? This was not a typical factory. Loom weaving was a dying skill. Machines had taken over for people. And in the rare cases where human skills were needed, production had been moved, as he intended, to China. Where would he find skilled artisans who were familiar with the antiquated looms?

He stopped himself. Was he just trying to make a case for Cassie? Were his personal feelings affecting his business decisions?

Hell, yes. Anyone else would have already received an ultimatum and been shown the door.

"This is ridiculous," Willa said. "You are wasting Mr. Axon's time."

He held up a hand to silence her. "What are your demands?" he asked Cassie.

"Give up the plant in China. Keep the jobs here."

He shook his head. He might be amenable to a demand for more severance, but did she really think he would abandon his intention so easily? "That's impossible."

Willa said, "The cost benefit will not—"

"So sell us the mill," Cassie said, interrupting her.

"What?" Willa asked.

Hunter looked at her intently and said, "Have you found a bank to finance the sale?"

She swallowed and glanced away. "We will."

Willa laughed. It was a shrill, almost piercing sound. "Axon Enterprises is not a bank."

"This isn't right," Cassie said, staring at him with burning, reproachful eyes. "You have no interest in running a mill, nor do you have any appreciation for the work that we do."

"Whether I appreciate it or not is beside the point," Hunter said calmly. "I bought it. And I own it."

"All you want is the Bodyguard patent. So take it. But give us back the mill."

He was silent for a moment. "Sell you the mill, but keep the patent?"

"That's right. You can go produce the patent in China. And we'll stay right here, making beautiful fabrics."

He sighed. He felt for her. He did. And he wanted to help her. But even well-meaning workers would not be able to keep this mill afloat. It had been hemorrhaging money for years. "What will that do? You'll still have a mill on the verge of bankruptcy."

"We'll take that chance."

"Cassie," Oliver said, appearing in the doorway. He looked shocked to see her there. "What are you doing?"

"I'm talking to your new boss," she said simply.

He took her by the arm. "Why are you doing this to me?"

Hunter's blood boiled at the sight of another man touching Cassie. Get your hands off her, he ached to say. Instead he said in a voice that commanded attention, "Let her speak."

Cassie shrugged her arm away from Oliver's grasp.

"We're not going down without a fight," she said, looking directly at Hunter. "We will not go back to work until you agree to our demands."

He did not like being threatened. "I can bring in others to do your jobs," he said.

"It will take time. Time which, we understand, you don't have."

Under any other circumstance, he would have been furious. He did not negotiate with soon-to-be-obsolete factory workers. But the frustration he felt toward the situation only seemed to fuel his desire for Cassie.

She crossed her arms, defiant. "We're not going to stop at the strike, either. We'll call the news media, we'll write letters to politicians…."

"The news media?" Willa said. "What news media?"

"The Albany stations."

Willa scoffed. "As if they care about a local-yokel mill an hour away."

"I'm not going to give up until you listen to me," Cassie said to Hunter. "I may not succeed but I can make this very, very difficult for you."

Willa took a step toward Cassie. "How dare you threaten Mr. Axon like that." She turned back toward Hunter and said, "I apologize for this insolence. I suggest you let me deal with this little insurgence."

Still looking at Cassie, Hunter said to Willa, "Will you give me a minute alone with Cassie, please?"

Willa said, "I think this is setting a poor example. If you kowtow to these ridiculous demands, any of them, it will hinder our efforts in other communities."

"I'll deal with Cassie," Hunter repeated through clenched jaws.

"Oh," Willa said, as if he had been communicating in code. "Alone. Right, I got it." Willa shot Cassie a nasty smile. "Of course, Hunter," she said. "Come along, Oliver."

When Oliver and Willa had left, Hunter took a step toward Cassie and said, "Sit down."

"No, thanks," she said.

He took another step toward her. "I wasn't asking you. I was telling you."

"Thanks for the explanation, but I wasn't confused."

"Yes," he said, "I think you are. This is not personal, Cassie. Whether you like it or not, I'm your boss. And you are costing me money."

"So fire me," she said.

"If I thought that would solve anything, I would. But I'm not about to give up the one degree of control I have."

This time it was Cassie's turn to step toward him. She looked up at him with anger smoldering in her eyes. "I don't care who you are. I'm not afraid of you. You can't control me."

It was a dare, plain and simple. But as he stared into Cassie's cool green eyes, his anger once again gave way to passion. She was wrong. He may not be able to control her mind but he damn well could control her body. He had done it before and was desperate to do it again. He wanted to take her in his arms, to make her sigh with pleasure and burn with desire.

"I see," he said. He swallowed and forced himself to turn away. "What are you offering?"

"What?"

"You're the mediator," he said. He glanced back at her. "You want to buy this mill. Tell your people to give me an offer."

"You'll consider it?"

He paused. "I'll consider just about anything."

She took a step backward and glanced away. But she was not quick enough. Hunter had seen the surprise in her eyes. She had not expected him to negotiate. So why was she doing this?

"I have to discuss this with my co-workers," she said.

"I'll give you twenty-four hours. You can present your proposal to my board."

"Tomorrow?"

Hunter thought he could detect a hint of panic. "Correct."

"Your board is coming here?"

"No," he said. "You're going to them."

"Where?"

"The Bahamas."

She paled, revealing a hint of despair. Normally he would

enjoy watching an antagonizer squirm. But not this time. He wanted to comfort her. To tell her everything would be all right.

"Be at the airport at noon tomorrow," he said. "My plane will be waiting."

She cleared her throat and asked, "Are we going together?"

"No," he said. "I'm leaving momentarily. After all, there's no reason for me to stay. Unless…"

"Unless what?"

"Unless you want me to."

He let his eyes gaze over her, drinking in her beauty.

She swallowed and touched the top button of her shirt as if making sure it was still closed. "No."

"So be it." He walked over to the door and opened it. "Until tomorrow."

She stood up and walked past him, accidentally brushing up against his arm as she passed. After she had left he shut the door and smiled. At that moment he would've been willing to sell her the mill for another night of passion.

Seven

By the time Cassie landed in Nassau it was nearly six. The attendant directed her out of the plane and toward the waiting limousine.

As she walked across the tarmac, she found herself shaking her head. It seemed unbelievable that she, Cassie Edwards, would be flying in a private plane and driving around in a limousine. After all, she was the girl who had to stick a hairbrush in her choke to start her car, the girl whose car engine leaked oil so badly she was forced to carry a case of oil and a can opener so she could add more at each destination.

She wondered what it would be like to be as rich as Hunter Axon. She knew that some people assumed there was no such thing as having too much money, but she disagreed. To some unfortunate souls, money was like a drug, intoxicating and overwhelming. The more they had, the more they wanted.

Like Oliver. He had been the richest man in Shanville, living a life that most just dreamed of. But it was not enough. And his quest for more cost him his company, his town and the people who loved him. She was certain that Oliver would one day discover that wealth could not buy him what he wanted most: happiness.

She couldn't help but compare Oliver to Hunter Axon. Hunter was intense, serious and ambitious. Not to mention one of the richest men in the country. But was he happy? He did not have a wife or children. But he had his pick of women, which, in and of itself, would probably be enough to make most men happy.

Cassie nervously licked her lips. She had to stop thinking of Hunter in such personal terms. He was her employer, her boss. End of subject. It did not matter if he was happy or unhappy.

She stepped inside the limousine and introduced herself to the driver. She then opened up her proposal and went over her notes one last time. After a grueling seven-hour meeting, the employees of Demion Mills had agreed on an offer. They would not try to buy back the patent. They couldn't afford it. But they would give Hunter more than a fair price for the mill. The deal, however, was dependent on his cooperation. They would make payments to him, forcing him to act as a bank.

She knew that the offer was not strong enough. But they had little choice. No bank would give them a loan. Their homes were their only collateral, and if the mill failed, their homes and land would be worthless.

So why would Axon Enterprises agree to such a scheme?

Once again she questioned their decision to go forward. Had Hunter been right? Would they have been better off just quietly accepting the severance?

Perhaps. But Cassie couldn't shake the feeling that they still had a chance of saving their company. For, despite what she had heard about Hunter Axon's ruthlessness, she had seen other qualities in him as well. She was almost certain that beneath the veneer of invulnerability was the man she had seen the first night they met: sensitive, protective and caring.

But were her personal feelings affecting her perception?

As much as she hated to admit it, she still felt a connection to him. She was certain she always would. After all, he was the first man with whom she had made love. And nothing would ever change that.

The driver slowed down. Cassie suddenly realized they were not at an office, but a home. As they approached, the iron gates at the end of the driveway swung open.

They drove down the long, curving drive. The house, invisible from the road, loomed ahead. It was exactly what she had imagined—a rambling Spanish-style mansion that, with its manicured grounds, resembled a country club.

She half expected to see the flurry of activity that was typical of great estates: gardeners, maids and butlers rushing around. But there was none of that. In fact, it seemed serenely quiet and deserted. Cassie stepped out of the limousine as the front door opened. Instead of a uniformed butler, a plain-faced, middle-aged woman in jeans and a T-shirt stood at the doorway and smiled. "Come on in," she said. "Mr. Axon is out back."

Cassie paused inside the cavernous entrance. Huge oil paintings, two stories high, filled the foyer. A large sweeping staircase straight from Tara wrapped its way toward the sky.

Cassie followed the woman through the French doors at the far end of the hall and out to the patio.

It was a view out of a magazine. Lush green acres rolling down to a white sandy beach and the green water of the Atlantic. Off to the right, stone lions guarded an infinity swimming pool.

Hunter was sitting at a table on the veranda, his back toward her.

He glanced up as Cassie approached.

"Hello, Mr. Axon," she said.

The term "Mr. Axon" brought a slight smile to his face. He stood up and held out his hand. He didn't look as if he was dressed for a business meeting. The brown hair that had been slicked back in Shanville was curly and natural. He was wearing an outfit similar to the one he had worn their first night together, a soft linen shirt tucked into linen pants. "Miss Edwards."

She took his hand. Once again he held it as though he wasn't about to let go. And part of her wished he wouldn't. She gave herself a mental slap. Focus. She pulled away. "Where is everyone?"

"You mean the board?"

She nodded.

"We have to go to them." Still looking at her, he asked, "Are you ready?"

She nodded. "I hope so."

"Good." He nodded toward the setting sun. "I had hoped to do it today, but because of the delay in your arrival, I bumped it to tomorrow morning."

Which left…the night. And she had not made hotel reservations. As if reading her mind, he said, "I took the liberty of making reservations for you at a hotel around the corner. I think you'll find it has all the amenities you need."

And she had no doubt it cost a fortune, as well. She had investigated all the hotels on her last visit. Nothing was as inexpensive as the Barter Hotel.

"Thank you," she said, "But I prefer the hotel I stayed in the last time."

"Ah," he said. "The Barter Hotel by any chance?"

She nodded. How did he know that?

"It's closed temporarily."

"But I was just there."

"They're renovating."

"Oh," she said, disappointed.

"Of course, you're welcome to stay here. I have several guest rooms."

She shook her head. "No. No, thank you."

He nodded. She could see a twinkle in his eyes. Was he teasing her?

"In that case," he said, glancing at his watch, "I'll see you to the car."

"I'm leaving?"

When he paused, she glanced away. What was wrong with her? She had sounded disappointed, as if she had wanted to stay with him. For good reason. As much as she hated to admit it, she *was* disappointed.

"I'm afraid I have dinner plans this evening."

His news took her breath away. Dinner plans? With whom?

She tried to ignore the jealousy ripping through her heart. What did she expect? She was not dating him. She had merely slept with him. But if he had dinner plans, why would he invite her to spend the night?

Was he willing to go out to dinner with another woman and return home to sleep with her?

"Unfortunately it's an engagement I cannot cancel," he said, turning away as if dismissing her.

"I wouldn't expect you to," she said coldly. Hmph! What did she care if he had a date? He was free to see whomever he liked.

Right? Right!

The thin veneer of anger could not hide the deep well of despair.

But she was not allowed to feel despair. Nor was she allowed to feel territorial. She barely knew Hunter.

She swallowed her emotions as he led her through the house and back to the limo, where the driver stood outside her door, waiting. Hunter said, "I hope you enjoy your stay at the hotel. Everything is taken care of, so feel free to order anything you like from the room service menu."

"That's not necessary," she said. "I have my own money."

"My company has a suite of rooms at the hotel, permanently reserved for visitors," he said. "We have never charged a guest."

"Oh," she said. "Well then, thank you."

"I'll see you tomorrow morning," he said, slamming her door.

Hours later Hunter was once again staring out over the water. He shook his head as he remembered the expression on his comptroller's face at dinner when he had informed him that he was thinking about selling the mill to its employees. "Are you crazy?" the man had asked.

Hunter had not seen the offer, but he knew it would not be titillating enough to convince his staff. After all, the risk was so significant no bank would finance the loan. There was no way the workers could afford to offer him enough to make it worth his while.

"So why?" the comptroller had asked. "Why would you even consider this?"

Hunter had not answered his question. After all, what could he say? That he was smitten with one of the women who wanted to buy it? It seemed ridiculous. He barely knew Cassie.

But the mere thought of her was enough to bring a smile to his lips. He remembered the way she had walked into his office, her arms crossed, her beautiful face turned up in defiance. She had been wearing her work attire as if to remind him of who she was: Cassie Edwards, factory worker. What she didn't realize was that he didn't care whether she was a photographer or a factory worker. He was not impressed by fancy titles and clothes. Even external beauty rarely moved him. His attraction to Cassie was based on something else, something he couldn't define. A quality or qualities that, when put together, made her the most intriguing woman he had ever met.

But was that reason enough to give her what she wanted?

No. Intellectually he knew that selling the workers back the mill would be a mistake. But he had to consider it. He couldn't bear the thought of disappointing Cassie, a woman he barely knew. But was she worth the risk?

He needed another opinion. So tomorrow he would take Cassie to his board. And if his board approved, well then, so be it. Regardless of his future with Cassie, he would give her what she wanted.

Eight

Cassie brushed the bread crumbs off her skirt as she stared out the limousine window. She usually skipped breakfast, but today she had made an exception. She was presenting her offer to Hunter's board and she certainly didn't want her stomach growling in the middle of the presentation.

But her stomach was tied in such knots that she found it almost impossible to eat the large breakfast that had appeared at her door that morning, "Compliments of Mr. Axon." She had choked down a piece of toast and swallowed a few sips of coffee before heading out the door.

She tapped her fingers nervously on her legs. She had hardly slept the night before and she was certain she looked as tired as she felt. She had stayed up, tossing and turning, her mind going a million miles a minute.

She had every reason to be nervous. After all, she had never given a business presentation before. She did not know what to expect.

As much as she wished that that alone was responsible for her insomnia, the truth of the matter lay elsewhere. She didn't want to admit it, but she couldn't stop thinking about Hunter. How could he have invited her to spend the night at his house when he had a dinner date with someone else?

Was he trying to make her jealous? She doubted it. If he felt anything for her at all, it was lust, plain and simple.

But what did she care? So their one-night stand had turned into just that. That was what she had intended, right?

But she had not expected to see him again. She had expected to return home with a beautiful memory of a kind and gentle man. And now that she knew who he was...well, the beautiful memory had turned into an embarrassment. Instead of feeling grateful for the time they shared, she felt guilty. It was as if she had done something wrong. Something illicit. And she had. Instead of protecting her friends from Hunter Axon, she had slept with him.

And for some terrible reason, she wanted to do it again.

Ugh. What was wrong with her? How could she even think such a thing?

The limousine stopped at a red light. Cassie glanced out the window. They were approaching Hunter's estate. She swallowed and stared at the beautiful palm trees lining both sides of the street. Suddenly something caught her eye. It was a brightly colored bird, unlike any she had ever seen before.

She instinctively reached for her camera, but for the first time she could remember, her camera was not there. She had purposely not brought it. She was pretending to be a corporate executive, and an executive would not walk into a meeting with a camera slung around her neck.

Cassie's stomach growled. She patted it and sighed. It was hopeless.

As they approached the entrance to Hunter's estate, the iron gates swung open once again and the limousine drove down the long, narrow driveway. The driver stopped in front of Hunter's house and hurried out to open her door.

Cassie stepped out of the limousine and, after thanking her

driver, clutched her folder against her chest and strode up the steps. Just as she was raising her hand to knock, the door opened.

The woman who had answered the door the day before appeared in front of her. She greeted Cassie pleasantly and once again led her through the house and out the back. Hunter was outside, talking on the phone.

He was not dressed as she might have expected. He was wearing the most casual outfit he had worn so far: khaki Bermuda shorts and a short-sleeved linen shirt.

What was going on? "Is the meeting canceled?" she asked.

"No," he said. Perhaps it did not matter what he wore. After all, he was the boss. And maybe the dress code for professionals in the Bahamas was different from in the States.

If that was the case, then once again she was dressed inappropriately. She was wearing a vintage suit she had found at a flea market—a simple cotton skirt and a sleeveless silk blouse topped by a tight-fitting cotton blazer.

As the heat crept up her cheeks, Hunter smiled sweetly, putting her fears to rest. "You look nice."

She couldn't help but appreciate the gesture. "Thanks," she said.

"All right," he said. "Let's go." With that, he turned and began to walk toward the water.

"Isn't the car that way?" she asked, motioning behind her.

"Yes," he said, continuing to walk.

She hurried to catch up with him. "I don't understand."

"We're traveling by boat," he said, nodding toward the cigarette boat in front of them.

"A boat?" Now she really was confused. "I just assumed we were going to your office."

"We're meeting at an island offshore," he said, jumping aboard. Like his yacht, the boat looked brand-new. Hunter said, "You might want to take those shoes off. And, uh, the stockings as well."

She just looked at him. The stockings?

As if reading her mind, he shrugged and said, "You're welcome to keep them on if you like but this deck is slick. I know you wouldn't want to end up in the water before your presentation."

She glanced down. How in the world would she get her panty hose off? Was it possible to do it and somehow keep her dignity? No. She'd just have to take her chances.

"It's all right," she said. She held on to the rail and hopped on. The minute her feet hit the deck of the boat she felt them give way. In that split second she knew that Hunter had been right. It was no time for a swim.

But before she hit the water, he grabbed her. He swung her around as if she were no heavier than a feather. He held her close. Looking in her eyes he said, "You might want to reconsider your decision."

"My decision?" she murmured. What decision was he referring to? Her decision to spend the night alone in a hotel room when she could've been snuggled up next to him?

He leaned forward, and for a split second she thought he was going to kiss her. Instead he righted her and, glancing at her panty hose, said, "You can take them off below if you prefer."

She nodded. He slowly removed his hands. As he turned the key in the ignition, she went below, where she took off her panty hose, rolled them up and stuck them in her purse.

She took off her jacket and walked back up, barefoot and sleeveless. She sat down next to him.

He was idling the boat in the water. "Ready?"

She nodded.

"Hold on," he said. He revved the engine, and with a start, they took off across the water.

"Isn't this a little unorthodox?'" she asked over the din of the engine.

"What do you mean?"

"Taking a boat to a board meeting."

He shrugged his shoulders. "I don't like doing things by the book."

The boat seemed to glide across the water. They were headed straight into the Atlantic. Up to the left, Cassie could see a school of dolphins. "Look," she said, excited. She pointed them out to Hunter.

He slowed the boat down. When she glanced at him, she saw that he was looking not at the dolphins but at her. "Was the hotel suitable?" he asked.

She nodded and turned back toward the dolphins. "Great," she said. "Thanks for breakfast."

She glanced sideways at him. Once again she found herself wondering about his evening. Whom had he spent it with? "What about you?" she asked.

"What do you mean?"

"I remember you said you had dinner plans."

He nodded. "Oh, yes." He glanced back at her. "It was a long night."

A long night. She got it. He wanted her to know that he'd slept with her. Whoever she was.

How dare he? How could he be so narcissistic as to assume that she would even care—

The boat hit a wave straight on. Water splashed against her silk blouse, making it cling to her skin. Her bra was clearly visible. Not exactly the kind of outfit you wanted to wear on a boat, beside a man with whom you had just slept, a man who was now sleeping with someone else. But that was the least of her worries.

"Sorry," Hunter said. "It's choppier than I thought." She saw his eyes glance toward her chest. He nodded toward the back. "There's a towel back there."

She grabbed the towel and wrapped it around her. When she sat back down, he pointed toward the island they were approaching. "That's where we're going."

"But…it looks almost deserted."

"It is. Almost."

He drove up to an old dock. He turned off the boat and began securing it to the dock.

"Where are we meeting your board?"

"Right there," he said, pointing to an old rambling shack on the beach.

"There?" she asked, more surprised than horrified. "In that hut?"

He grinned.

"What is this, Hunter?" she asked. "What's going on?" This had to be some sort of joke. Where was the fancy marina? Where were the hotels? Where were the conference rooms? "You promised me—"

"I promised you an opportunity to meet my board. My board consists of one person—the only person whose advice I trust. My father. This is where he lives." He held out his hand. "That man there," he said, nodding behind him, "is the man who will decide your future."

She glanced toward the shore. The man approaching them was wearing a bright Hawaiian shirt with blue-jean shorts. His gray, bushy hair was partially covered by a baseball cap. He waved and smiled.

"Don't let his sweet-old-man demeanor fool you," Hunter said. "He's every bit as mean and tough as I am."

"Your father?"

"That's right."

"Why didn't you tell me?"

"Does it matter?" he asked. "If you had asked me who was on my board I would've been happy to tell you." He nodded toward her purse and her folder. "Now, why don't you hand those down to me so you can meet him."

Cassie glanced at her belongings. It seemed ridiculous to bring a purse on the beach. She pulled out her shoes and handed her folder to Hunter.

"Morning," Hunter's father said. He held out his hand to Cassie, helping her off the boat. "You must be Cassie. Hunter's told me all about you."

Cassie glanced at Hunter. "Really?"

"Yep," his father said. "You're every bit as pretty as he claimed."

She saw Hunter wince. "Let's keep it professional, Dad. Remember, this isn't a social visit."

Hunter had described her as pretty? She couldn't help but feel pleased.

"Whatever you say," his father replied with a big grin.

Cassie smiled in return. As she glanced at the older man's friendly smile, she could feel her apprehension fade. He seemed to radiate sincerity. "It's nice to meet you, Mr. Axon."

"Phil. Call me Phil."

"Hey, Phil," said Hunter. He nodded toward the cottage. "Are we meeting at the house?"

"Inside?" he asked. "On such a beautiful day?"

It was beautiful. Cassie glanced at the sky. Eighty degrees and sunny, with not a drop of humidity.

"I was hoping," Phil continued, "that we might be able to discuss things over a pole."

"Excuse me?" Cassie asked.

"I don't think Cassie is interested in fishing, Dad."

"Actually," Cassie said, "I would love to." She still wasn't sure if Hunter had been telling her the truth when he said the future of the mill rested in the hands of his board—his father. But if her fate really did rest in the hands of this seemingly kind and simple man, then so be it. Perhaps she still had a chance of saving the mill after all.

Phil smiled and held out his arm. Cassie looped her hand through it and together they walked toward an embankment at the top of which were four chairs.

It didn't take Cassie long to start talking about Shanville and Demion Mills. She told Hunter's father the story of how the mill began and described how it had become the anchor of the town. She told him about the looms and explained how they hand wove the material. She talked about the people who worked there and explained why their futures were dependent on the mill.

Hunter's father listened patiently. When she was finished, Phil asked her the same question Hunter had asked. "What makes you think you can save it?"

She looked at Hunter. "I'm not sure I can. But I know I have to try."

He shrugged. "Fair enough." He glanced at Hunter. "How much of a hit will you take?"

"He's keeping the patent," Cassie said defensively, before Hunter could answer. "We're just asking him to finance the buy-back."

Hunter raised his eyebrows. "The mill has not made a profit in five years."

Phil maintained eye contact with his son. "So this is not a business decision, is it?"

Cassie swallowed. Perhaps she had been wrong about Phil Axon's understanding nature. She said, "We'll pay him back regardless. Even if we have to sell our homes to do it."

Hunter said to his father, "You and I can talk about this later."

"There's nothing to talk about."

"What?" both Hunter and Cassie asked simultaneously.

Phil glanced at his son. "I think she's a woman of her word. If she says she'll pay you back, then she'll pay you back."

"With interest," Cassie said.

Hunter glanced away, obviously surprised by his father's proclamation. Before he had a chance to respond, however, his phone rang. He flipped it open and turned away as he spoke in a low voice.

Cassie looked at Phil and smiled. "Thank you," she said.

"You're more than welcome. But I think you should know it's ultimately Hunter's decision."

"Then," she said wistfully, "I doubt we stand a chance."

"I disagree."

She gave him a puzzled look.

"I understand why you might say that. I know his reputation. The corporate robber baron. And I'm not saying it's not deserved. But I know a different side."

She glanced away.

"You know," his father said, "life hasn't been easy for Hunter. Not easy at all. After his mother died, I went through a hard time. Things just got worse when I lost my job. I came here to figure things out. My mother—Hunter's grandmother—was worried about us living out here alone. She didn't have much faith in my ability to bring up a child. And I suppose she was right. I could barely take care of myself.

"We never had much money," he continued. "I did my best,

but I was dependent on the sea. Sometimes the fish were plentiful, sometimes they weren't. We never had any extra money for books, clothes, medicine, the stuff most kids take for granted."

Hunter's father was a nice man who obviously loved his son. But how could he excuse Hunter's behavior? Lots of children grew up poor. They didn't turn into money-hungry tycoons.

"One year Hunter's grandma got sick. She'd never been in good shape. Well, we put her in the boat and got her over to the mainland. But we waited and waited for them to check her into the hospital. In the meantime, we kept watching all these other people just walk right in and get service. See, it didn't matter if she was dying. We were poor. They took the ones with money or insurance first. By the time we finally got in, it was too late. She died. They tried to save her, but they couldn't. Hunter was convinced if we'd had money, things would've turned out differently."

"I'm sorry," she said.

"His goals were commendable. He was driven not by greed but by compassion."

She didn't answer. She did not want to be the one to tell him that honorable intentions did not necessarily make an honorable man. But still, she couldn't help but be touched by Hunter's history. If her grandmother had suffered the same fate, who knew what impression that might have made on her?

"How did he end up at Yale?"

"After his grandma died, Hunter applied to a boarding school. He got in, and when he graduated he applied to the best of schools, determined to work his way through college." He smiled. "He's done it all by himself, every step of the way."

She understood why he would be proud. It was an impressive feat—a boy of simple means turning himself into one of the richest men in the country.

Phil shrugged. "I know I'm rambling."

"Not at all," she said with a smile.

He looked back at the water. "I must say, when Hunter told me he was bringing a lady out here I just assumed it was a date. He doesn't often bring his associates."

She glanced at Hunter. He was still talking on the phone, his back to them, oblivious to the conversation occurring behind him. She felt a pang of jealousy. Did he bring dates often? How many women had he brought to meet his father?

As if reading her mind, Phil said, "Although I don't know why I'd think it was anything but a business associate, I can't remember the last time he brought a girlfriend out here."

She breathed a sigh of relief. But what did she care? She was not dating him. Phil said, "He's a good man, my Hunter."

She glanced down. A good man? He was a powerful man, a man who had made millions. But he was not exactly known for his philanthropic nature. Then again, from what Phil had just told her, she could understand why he might think such a thing. "I've always felt the one thing my son needed was a good woman."

"I don't think your son has any trouble finding women."

"Just not the right one." He shook his head. "He thought he found her once."

"What do you mean?" Cassie asked, stabbed by a momentary pang of jealousy.

"He was going to marry her. Darn near broke his heart, she did. I tried to warn him. Saw it coming a mile away." He shrugged. "But he's always had a mind of his own."

"Well," Hunter said, appearing behind him, "what did I miss?" Cassie glanced up at him. Hunter had suffered a broken heart? She found it difficult to imagine. She had just assumed him to be the heartbreaker, not the other way around.

"Oh, we're just getting to know each other. Right, Cassie?" Phil asked with a wink.

She nodded.

"Cassie," Phil said, "it seems a shame to go back to the mainland so soon. Would you like to see the island?"

She glanced at Hunter, who looked at his watch. She picked up on his cue and said, "I'm not sure we have time."

"Come on now, Hunter," Phil said. "She's come a long way. And it's lunchtime."

"All right," Hunter reluctantly agreed.

Phil smiled. "You should take her to the fishmonger." He shrugged. "The island only has one decent restaurant and it's not much."

"Aren't you coming?" Cassie asked hesitantly. The only reason she had been amenable to staying was that she thought *he* was inviting her.

"Me?" he asked, as if the thought had never occurred to him. "I've got too much work to do. But you two go on."

"Too much work?" Hunter asked, surprised.

"You got it," Phil said. "Now go on."

Hunter rolled his eyes.

Cassie stood up. "I'm not exactly dressed for an island tour."

"Leave your shoes here. Besides that, you're fine."

"My shoes?" Cassie repeated.

Hunter shrugged. "People rarely wear shoes on the island."

"I'll hold on to them for you," Phil said. "Don't you worry."

As they walked away, Hunter whispered, "Don't let my dad pressure you. You don't have to do this if you don't want to. I can take you back."

She glanced around. The sweet smell of jasmine filled the air. She could feel her resolve weaken. After all, how often did she travel to an island paradise? "No," she said. "I would like to stay. If, of course, it's okay with you."

"My schedule is clear for the day."

She nodded. Once again she found herself wondering why Hunter had brought her there. "I like your dad," she said. "He seems like a nice man."

"He is."

She stopped walking. "Does his opinion really make a difference?"

"Not typically," he said, without looking away.

Any optimism she might have felt disappeared with his words. She swallowed hard, trying not to reveal her frustration. "So, why am I here?"

"Because," he said, "this is not a typical situation."

PLAY THE
Lucky Key Game

and you can get

FREE BOOKS
and a FREE GIFT!

Do You
Have the
LUCKY
KEY?

Scratch the gold areas with a coin. Then check below to see the books and gift you can get!

YES!

I have scratched off the gold areas. Please send me the **2 FREE BOOKS** and **GIFT** for which I qualify. I understand I am under no obligation to purchase any books, as explained on the back of this card.

326 SDL D39U

225 SDL D4AC

FIRST NAME   LAST NAME

ADDRESS

APT.#   CITY

STATE/PROV.   ZIP/POSTAL CODE

2 free books plus a free gift

1 free book

2 free books

Try Again!

Offer limited to one per household and not valid to current
Silhouette Desire® subscribers. All orders subject to approval.
Credit or Debit balances in a customer's account(s) may be offset
by any other outstanding balance owed by or to the customer.

DETACH AND MAIL CARD TODAY!

If offer card is missing write to: Silhouette Reader Service, 3010 Walden Ave., P.O. Box 1867, Buffalo NY 14240-1867

BUSINESS REPLY MAIL
FIRST-CLASS MAIL   PERMIT NO. 717-003   BUFFALO, NY

POSTAGE WILL BE PAID BY ADDRESSEE

SILHOUETTE READER SERVICE
3010 WALDEN AVE
PO BOX 1867
BUFFALO NY 14240-9952

NO POSTAGE
NECESSARY
IF MAILED
IN THE
UNITED STATES

"So you're honestly considering my proposal?" she said, as hope once again filled her heart.

"You wouldn't be here if I wasn't." His expression stilled and grew serious. He looked as if he was waiting for her to speak. But what did he want her to say?

He glanced away and nodded toward a small motorbike next to the house. "This is our transportation."

"That?" she said, looking at the bike. There was barely room for one person, not to mention two.

He jumped on. "Climb on," he said, turning the key to the ignition.

Cassie hesitated. Hunter met her eyes, as if daring her. He said, "You wanted to see the island. This is how people travel here."

She hiked up her skirt and sat behind him. Her bare legs rested against his.

"Hold on," he said.

As the bike jolted forward, she instinctively grabbed on to Hunter's waist. Through his shirt she could feel his taut muscles. Once again she saw his naked body, towering above her as he penetrated deep inside her. At the memory she stiffened slightly and leaned back.

They were traveling down a narrow dirt road carved out of a jungle. She could see glimpses of island life—brightly colored birds, the deep blue Atlantic. Finally they came out into a clearing. It was as if she had stepped back in time. Vendors of exotic fruit and fish crowded the streets. Although there was a small marina, it was wooden and rickety.

"This is the island that time has forgotten," Hunter said, stopping the bike in front of a small building.

"I'm surprised that some big resort hasn't gobbled this up yet."

"No," he said. "It's not going to happen, either."

"I wouldn't be too sure." She glanced at him. But she could tell by the expression on his face that he was not making an educated guess. He knew for a fact this island was safe from development. "You own this island, don't you?"

He held back a grin. "Let's eat."

So he owned an island, too. "I'm surprised you haven't sold it off to a developer. I bet you could make some money."

He stopped. "Believe it or not, I'm not all about money."

"Prove it."

"If I was all about money, you wouldn't be here right now." He was towering above her. His voice was low and his eyes were cold.

He held her gaze for a moment before turning and opening the door. The bright sunlight disappeared. They were in a small, dark room with a long bar behind which a man was grilling fish.

Hunter nodded toward a stool. "Have a seat."

"Hunter!" the man said, beaming when he saw him. "This is a surprise."

"I was in the neighborhood," Hunter said.

"I talked to your father," the man said. "He tells me you're very busy these days." The man looked at Cassie and smiled again. "I can see why."

Hunter raised an eyebrow. "I'm afraid you're wrong." He glanced at Cassie. "She thinks I'm an arrogant bastard."

The man looked at Cassie and frowned.

Embarrassed, she said, "I never said—"

"I didn't say you did. I said you thought it." She could see the mischievous twinkle in his eye. "Freddy, I'd like you to meet Cassie Edwards, a business associate."

"Nice to meet you, Miss Edwards," Freddy said with a smile. He grasped her hand warmly. "But you're wrong about this man here. He's the most decent man I've ever met."

"I think you give me a little too much credit, Freddy. But thank you."

Freddy chuckled. "I'll give you two the specials. It will fix you right up."

She glanced at Hunter. He was obviously still tickled by his own joke. "I enjoyed talking to your father. He's not what I would've expected," she said, as Freddy chopped a head off a fish. She looked away.

"How so?"

Who would think the father of a corporate giant would be so down to earth and nice? "He seems so…perceptive."

"He can be," Hunter said.

As they ate their meal, Hunter glanced at the woman beside him. He had enjoyed introducing her to his family and friends and the island he still referred to as home. Hunter turned back toward Freddy. He had known him his whole life. The two had grown up together, attended the local school, graduated in the same class. Although Hunter had never told another soul, it was he who had bought Freddy this restaurant. He had offered to set him up anyplace in the world he desired but Freddy had not wanted to move. He confessed his dream had always been to have a little restaurant right there on the beach. And so, that was exactly what Hunter had given him. But it was his friend who had made the restaurant a success.

"What about dessert?" Freddy asked when they were finished.

Cassie shook her head. "No thanks. That was delicious, though."

Freddy smiled and flashed Hunter the thumbs-up. Hunter could see Cassie turn red with embarrassment. "I like her!" Freddy said.

"Don't get too excited there," Hunter said. "Like I said, she's a business associate."

Freddy winked. "Well, maybe your business associate would like to see Blind Man's Peak."

"I don't think so," Hunter said, looking at her. "She needs to get back to the mainland."

"What's Blind Man's Peak?" she asked.

"We used to go there as kids. It's on top of an old volcano. It's got a view of all the islands around here."

"Sounds interesting."

What did that mean? Did she want to go? "It's a little bit of a hike. The path is too steep for the bike."

She put her napkin on her plate. "I can handle it."

"You can't go in bare feet."

"So let's go get my shoes."

"You can't wear high heels, Cassie. You could break something."

"Shoes? Does someone need shoes?" asked Freddy.

"Freddy…" began Hunter.

"What size?"

She smiled at Freddy. "Nine."

"Big feet," he said. "I'll be right back."

"Don't tell me he's gone out to find a pair of shoes for me."

"I'm afraid so."

"They sell shoes?"

He nodded. "Freddy has a big family. Most of them work in the vendor stands you saw out front. You could purchase a whole new wardrobe, if you like."

Freddy burst back in the front door. He ran over to the grill and flipped some more fish. Then he turned back toward Cassie and said, "Try these."

He handed her a pair of flip-flops on which someone had painstakingly glued shells. She said, "They're much too beautiful to wear."

"That's what they're for," Freddy argued.

She slipped them on. "They're wonderful. Thank you."

"Anything for a friend of Hunter's."

Hunter smiled appreciatively. "Thanks, Freddy."

Freddy winked and handed Hunter a pair of plain flip-flops. "I didn't want you to feel bad."

"I owe you one, my friend," Hunter said with a grin.

Hunter turned back toward Cassie. "Whenever you're ready…"

"I'm ready." She stood up. "Thank you for this delicious lunch," she said to Freddy. "And," she said, pointing to her feet, "for the shoes."

Hunter led Cassie out. They were almost to the door when Freddy once again flashed him a thumbs-up. Hunter was not surprised by his friend's opinion of Cassie. Nor was he surprised by his father's. It only cemented what he had suspected.

Cassie was not like Lisa.

He had taken Lisa to the island only once. Despite her kind words and pleasant smile, she had been all too anxious to escape back to the mainland and the comforts of an expensive hotel.

He got on the bike. Cassie jumped on behind him. She slid back as far as possible, but she could not stop her breasts from pushing up against him. She held her hands stiff, barely touching his waist.

He drove off the road, heading toward a familiar path. After a while they came out at another clearing. Hunter parked his bike. "We have to walk from here."

It had been years since Hunter had walked along this narrow dirt path. He had once made the trip at least once a day, but after he left the island, his trips were limited to an annual visit at best.

"Are you okay?" he asked Cassie, glancing at her flip-flops.

"Fine," she said.

He smiled to himself. He was impressed. Most women would never have agreed to such an adventure. Especially when dressed in a fancy skirt and blouse. But Cassie did not seem to care what she was wearing. She seemed completely at ease, as if taking a walk to the edge of a volcano was a typical outing.

"It's right up here," Hunter said.

Cassie passed him, climbing up the peak. The crater had long since filled in, leaving just a grassy, narrow knoll. "It's beautiful," she said, looking at the blue-green Atlantic and the islands dotting the sea.

He nodded as he stood beside her. "I used to come here a lot."

"Did you grow up on this island?"

He nodded. "I grew up in that 'hut,' as I believe you described it."

Cassie swallowed as the color drained out of her face. "I'm sorry," she said. "I didn't mean to insult you. I thought it was a cute house. I should've said bungalow."

The look on her face made Hunter regret he had even mentioned it. Cassie was not a snob. It was his own clumsy way of proving that he wasn't, either. "I know," he said.

She nodded, seemingly relieved.

"You think it looks small now," he said. "You should've seen it when my grandmother was alive." He rolled his eyes and laughed. Out of the corner of his eye he could see her smile.

"Your grandmother lived there, too?"

"Yes. She took the bedroom and my father the couch, and I had a mattress on the floor."

"You're kidding?"

He shook his head. "No. We didn't have much money. But my grandmother kept it together. You'd be surprised how far she could stretch one fish."

"My grandmother was the same way," she said. "She could stretch one pot roast a week." She smiled.

"What about you?"

"Me?" She shook her head. "I can't cook. I never felt the urge to try."

"You'd rather be out taking pictures."

She grinned. "I guess." They walked in silence for a while. Hunter couldn't help but think about her interest in photography. If Cassie did not have the mill, would she pursue a career behind the camera?

"What happened to your mother?" she asked.

"She died soon after I was born. My dad couldn't cope, so my grandmother came out from France to help. She raised me."

"Right," she said, flashing him a bright smile. "I remember now."

"What?"

"Say something in French."

He hesitated. *"Tu es la femme la plus belle que j'ai jamais vu,"* he said quietly. You are the most beautiful woman I have ever seen.

"What does that mean?"

"It means…" He paused and glanced up at the sky. "I hope it doesn't rain."

She nodded as if she didn't quite believe him. He shrugged and glanced away.

"Do you still have relatives in France?"

"Distant. My grandmother wanted to be buried back there, so I met some of them at her funeral."

"That must have been interesting."

"It was deafening."

"What?"

"We're a very loud family."

She laughed, and he felt his spirits soar.

She glanced back toward the water. "This is so beautiful. It feels like we're on the top of the world."

"That's why I loved it here. I could spend the day working and get home exhausted. But when I came up here I forgot everything. I felt as if I could take over the world."

She paused a minute. "Why are you telling me all this?" she asked quietly, a slight hesitation in her voice.

Why was he? He was getting personal. He couldn't seem to help himself. He wanted to open up to her, to prove to her he was not the bastard she thought he was. But there was only one way to do that.

"Hunter?" she said, still waiting for an answer.

"Cassie, I have to tell you, selling the mill to you does not make sense."

He could see her stiffen.

"But I'm going to accept your offer."

Her eyes opened wide in astonishment. "You are?"

He nodded. "I am."

"So the mill will stay open?"

"That's right."

"Why?"

Why? Wasn't it obvious? Because he couldn't stand the thought of disappointing her.

Instead he said, "I didn't realize that there was going to be such an insurgence from the locals. That's not the way I do business."

She stood still, almost as if she was afraid to breathe. "And you'll still produce the Bodyguard cloth in China?"

Why had she brought up the patent? Was she insinuating that she wanted the patent, too? A mill that size could never handle the production of a mass-market product.

"That was the deal." He could feel his defenses rise. He was angry. Didn't she understand that this was a financial risk that he would never have assumed in any other circumstance? He was not a bank that reached out to nonprofit clients. He bought companies. He didn't save them. "There will be some conditions of the sale, however," he said, taking a step back. "After all, I need to know that my investment will be returned."

"Of course," she said. Her arms were crossed in front of her chest. She was looking everywhere but at him. What had happened? Shouldn't she be happy? After all, he just gave her back the mill.

In any case, it was clear the cliff had lost its magic.

"Come on," he said. "Let's go."

Cassie barely said a word when they returned to his father's bungalow and retrieved her shoes, jacket and folder. She was polite and kind, but distant. Neither mentioned to his father that Hunter had agreed to sell the mill.

She was equally silent on the boat ride back. As they neared the dock, she finally said, "I'd like to return home as soon as possible."

Hunter glanced at her. "Okay."

"I have to get back and tell everyone the good news."

And Hunter had to deal with Willa. He knew she would not be pleased. She was already talking to museums about which items would be donated, looking forward to the large tax credit. And she had already taken several companies through who were interested in purchasing the space. She would immediately recognize that his selling the mill back to the workers was based on emotion rather than reason.

But he didn't care what Willa might think. At the moment all he could think about was Cassie.

He had half hoped that their rendezvous might suddenly turn romantic. But it hadn't. Even before he brought up the mill, Cassie had maintained her distance. It was as if she was purposely keeping him at arm's length. What had happened to the spontaneous woman he had met on the beach?

"I'll arrange your flight back," he said.

"Thank you," she said. "Will you be returning with me?"

"No." It was obvious that Cassie was only interested in a business relationship. Unfortunately, he was not willing or able to accept a platonic relationship. He could not be near her without wanting to touch her, without being tempted to kiss her.

Therefore, it was best if he stayed away from her. He would not return to Shanville. The lawyers would handle it from there.

"Tomorrow, then?" she asked.

He shook his head. "There's no reason to wait till tomorrow." He glanced at her. She was staring at him. "Is there?" he asked. Give me a reason, he pleaded silently. Please.

She shook her head. "I guess not."

His heart sank. He pulled up to the dock and stopped the boat. He stepped out and turned to offer her his hand. When she was safely on the dock, he let go.

He said, "I'll drive you to your hotel so you can gather your things. I'll let my office know that you'll be ready to leave in an hour."

"Wait," she said, stopping him.

He turned back toward her.

"I...I wanted to thank you."

"Sure," he said. "It's business, right?"

"No, it's not just business. You have been so kind. More than kind. I will always be grateful."

Her soft silk blouse fluttered in the wind. Her long auburn hair, tousled by the wind and water, was a mass of wild and sexy curls.

"Hunter," she said. Her emerald green eyes sparkled. "I think my first impression of you was correct."

"What was that?"

"That you were a kind and gentle man."

He smiled sadly. Unfortunately, that didn't seem to be enough. He turned and began walking toward the house.

"I don't want it to end like this," she said.

He stopped.

"I want to stay here tonight," she continued. "With you."

Nine

She said it. The words that had been floating in her head just came spilling out. And it was too late to take them back.

Not that she wanted to. In fact, she had meant every word.

She had been surprised by the turn of events. She had expected a stiff, informal board meeting, not a visit to his childhood home to meet his family and friends. She had been given a rare glimpse at the person behind the facade. Instead of a corporate jerk, she had found a man who still had a close relationship with his father and childhood friends, a man who had saved the island on which he had grown up.

He had a heart.

And up there on that cliff it had seemed as if he might have wanted to share it with her. In front of her eyes, he had metamorphosed back into the man she had originally met on the beach, the one who had split a coconut with his hands. The one with whom she had shared the most intimate of experiences.

But when he told her he was giving her back the mill, she could think of only one thing: returning to Shanville.

Why?

Because she had been frightened.

She was more terrified of Hunter, the man, than she had ever been of Hunter Axon, ruthless business tycoon.

It had taken a while to digest the information, taken a while to pump up her confidence. But ultimately she remembered that she had never run away from a challenge in her life. She was not about to start now.

And so she had offered to stay.

More than stay.

She had offered herself.

And from his reaction she could tell it was an offer he was not prepared to accept.

Hunter stood there, looking at her as if deciding what to do with her.

Perhaps, she thought, as her heart dropped, he had changed his mind. Perhaps she had misread the cues, the subtle signs of his interest. Perhaps she was wrong. Perhaps he didn't want her anymore.

The deal was done, the offer accepted. He was ready for her to go home.

He nodded, still looking at her. "Good," he said. Then he turned and began walking back toward the house.

Good? What did that mean?

As she hurried to catch up, Hunter swung open his phone. She could hear him arrange to have her things brought over from the hotel. That was that. He was about as excited as if she had offered him a bowl of soup.

"If it's not convenient for you, I can stay at the hotel," she said, still hurrying to keep up with him.

He stopped so short she almost ran into him.

"I don't like games," he said.

They were standing nose to nose, eye to eye. "Neither do I," she said.

"Then why are you playing them? If you want to stay here tonight, you're more than welcome. If not, I'll see to your return to Shanville."

Why was he being so cold and indifferent? Didn't he want her to stay? "If you don't want me here, I'll—" She stopped talking. His gaze had softened and he was looking at her tenderly.

He touched her cheek. His fingers trailed downward, outlining her chin. He gently lifted her head toward him and kissed her. It was deep and sensual, filled with a passion that belied his outward calm. Her senses reeled and her knees grew weak. Finally he said, "I've wanted to do that ever since I saw you in that auditorium."

He took her hand, walking more slowly now. "Unfortunately, I have some business to attend to. But it shouldn't take me long."

"That's fine," she said. "Is there a place where I can freshen up?"

He touched her hair. "You look beautiful," he said, practically caressing her with his eyes.

"Thanks," she said. "But I would love a shower."

He nodded. "We can arrange that." They entered through the back. He led her through his grand rooms and up the sweeping staircase. As she walked up the stairs, she admired the paintings hanging on the wall. Most were by contemporary artists she had studied in school. "Is this a Kandinsky?" she asked, stopping in front of a painting with brightly colored cubes.

He nodded. "Do you like modern art?"

"Sometimes," she replied honestly.

He smiled.

"But I can't imagine having art like this in my house. I'd be so worried."

"Worried?"

"What if there's a hurricane…what if there's a leak…?" She shrugged.

"It is a responsibility," he said. "I'll eventually donate most of these to a museum. In the meantime, I have a vault downstairs where I can put the paintings in case of a hurricane or leak."

He stood there, looking at her as he continued to hold her hand. He started to walk again, but more slowly. He took her into a room that looked like an expensive hotel suite. A king-size bed faced French doors that overlooked the pool and the Atlantic beyond. Off to the side were two comfortable-looking lounge chairs.

Like the rest of the house, it looked brand-new. "Please make yourself at home. In the bathroom there are toiletries, robes, towels…anything you might need. I'll see that you receive your things as soon as they arrive." He held her hand to his lips and kissed it. It was a chivalrous, gallant act that had the desired effect. It left her wanting more.

He turned and left, closing the door behind him. She closed her eyes, fighting off a sudden case of nerves. Was she sure about this?

Could she handle another night with Hunter? After all, she still hadn't quite recovered from the last one.

But she had little choice. In the argument between mind and body, her body was pulling rank.

One night. One more night.

And then she would be on a plane back to Shanville. She would be so busy she would forget all about her elusive lover. Right?

She walked into the bathroom. Like the rest of the house, it was grand, elegant and looked brand-new. White marble was everywhere, the countertop, the floor, the shower. Everything appeared to have been designed with women in mind—right down to the little basket of lilac-scented toiletries and the woman's robe.

She suddenly realized that this was not just any old guest room. This was exactly what it looked like: a suite reserved for his female guests.

But why would he give them a separate room? Why not have them use his private quarters?

She wondered how many women had used this room to "freshen up." Had the woman he'd gone out with the previous night used it, as well?

She glanced around the brightly colored walls. So what if she had? Cassie reminded herself that she could not think about the future or the past. She was there now, and that was all that mattered.

She scrubbed off the salt and sand, relaxing in the steamy heat of the shower. Afterward she wrapped herself in the fluffy robe and brushed her hair.

She stepped out of the bathroom. On the table between the

lounge chairs was an open bottle of champagne and a crystal glass. Someone had delivered it to her room while she had been in the shower.

She helped herself to a glass of champagne and walked out on the balcony.

She wondered whether she should dress in the same clothes she had worn to the island. After all, who knew when her clothes might arrive?

Then again, she thought, admiring the view, who cared? She was perfectly content to take a while to admire her beautiful surroundings and rehash the day's events.

But she didn't have long to wait. Within moments there was a knock on her door. When she opened it, Hunter himself was standing in front of her, carrying her suitcase.

She said, "I'm surprised you brought that up yourself."

"Why?"

"I thought you'd have one of your..." Servants? Helpers? "One of the people who work for you."

"The only person who works here is Gehta," he said, walking past her and setting the suitcase on the bed. He had showered as well, and his wet hair was slicked back. He had changed out of the clothes he had worn that day and was wearing a linen shirt and pants.

"And she's gone for the day," he continued. "I'd never ask her to carry it up those steps, anyway."

So they were alone. He was the one who had brought in the champagne.

"Are you enjoying the champagne?" he asked softly. She saw him swallow as his eyes slowly grazed down her body.

She nodded. "Yes, thank you."

He took another step toward her, staring into her eyes. He touched her cheek.

It was just a touch, but it was enough to cause her body to react. Maybe the champagne, the shower, the beautiful and warm evening were all to blame.

Still looking into her eyes, he undid the tie to her robe. He paused, as if waiting for her to stop him. But she didn't. All of her concerns faded away. All she could think about was how much she wanted him to touch her, to hold her. How much she wanted to feel him inside her.

He put his hands on her shoulders and gently pushed off her robe. It fell to the ground, leaving her naked and exposed.

He had not taken his eyes off hers. Usually she was modest and reserved, but there was something about Hunter that made her throw caution to the wind. She felt bold and passionate. Adventurous. She straightened her back, not afraid to display her body.

"You're so beautiful," he said again, gently touching her shoulders. His breathing became ragged and harsh, as if an electrical current ran through the air. She half expected him to pounce on her, to toss her down on the bed and take her hard and rough. He moved slowly, teasing her with time. One hand slid down her back and cupped her rear end. The other worked its way down her front, massaging her breasts before sliding down toward her belly. She breathed in his warm, musky scent as a current ran through her.

As he moved behind her, he placed a hand over her breast, gently encouraging her to relax against him. They were in front of the open window. "Look at the sun," he said as his right hand continued to explore. She forced herself to look outside. She felt the warm breeze against her bare body, felt the crispness of his linen shirt pressed against her back and his warm breath against her neck.

He caressed her gently, his fingers working their way down her belly. She inhaled sharply as he touched the delicate skin inside her thighs, making his way toward her most sensitive spot. Her thoughts fragmented as his fingers ran up the delicate arch and back down through the soft folds, giving her the most intimate of massages.

She raised her arms and wrapped them around the back of his head as she reveled in the pleasure that came from being rubbed and touched so sensuously.

Finally, she had no choice but to surrender. He held her tight as her body released, causing her to shudder in his arms. When she finished he turned her toward him and touched her hair. "Cassie," he said softly.

But she did not want him to speak. Not yet.

She began unbuttoning his shirt. She wanted to do for him what he had done for her. After his shirt she concentrated on his pants. She reached for him, taking him in her hands before bringing him to her lips.

She heard him moan slightly and felt his fingers run through her hair as if encouraging her to continue.

When she paused, he took the opportunity to lift her off her feet and carry her to the bed. As he stared into her eyes, she felt as if he were looking into her soul.

Their lovemaking was passionate, almost desperate. He held her hands as he moved deeper and deeper.

As the pleasure once again began to build, she arched her hips, bringing him deeper. She closed her eyes only when she felt her body begin to release. Hunter let go at the same time, joining her in a deep climax.

Afterward he pulled her to him, holding her close.

They lay there, their naked bodies wrapped around each other, quietly watching the sun sink into the sea.

When just a fringe of orange appeared above the water, he touched her hair. "You're warm."

"A little."

"Do you want to go for a swim?"

"I didn't bring a suit." It hadn't occurred to her. After all, technically she was here on business, not pleasure. But Demion Mills seemed worlds away.

"You don't need a suit," he said. "There's no one around."

He stood up and handed her a towel. It was a dare. And she accepted. But the brazenness she had experienced only moments earlier was gone. She felt vulnerable from their emotionally charged intimacy. She was too modest to walk around the house naked, people or no people. She wrapped the towel around her. "All right." He laughed, following suit and tying a towel around his waist.

He led her back down the grand staircase and through the open French doors. She paused before walking outside.

"No one will know," he said, kissing her shoulder. "We're alone."

He led her to the pool. Once again she felt as though she were at an exotic resort. The only light came from the moon, the blue-and-gold spotlights framing the palm trees and the lit, black-bottomed pool. Flashing her a mischievous grin, he dropped his towel and dove in. She watched him glide underwater, his form that of an experienced swimmer.

She dropped her towel as well and stood there for a moment, enjoying the tropical breeze. He reached the end of the pool and glanced back toward her, motioning for her to join him.

She held her nose and jumped. But she didn't hit bottom. In the flash of a second he was there. He caught her in the water and swung her up in his arms. "Do you do this often?" she asked as he lifted her above the water.

"Do what?"

"Skinny-dipping."

"Actually, I don't think I've ever even been in this pool."

"What? How long have you lived here?"

"Years. But I'm fairly certain I've never used the pool."

"Why not?"

He shrugged. "I don't know. I guess I'm always working."

"I know you have time to date," she said. "Even the women of Shanville know that."

"Really?" he said. "Well, I'm flattered the women of Shanville care so much about my personal life."

"So none of your women ever wanted to go swimming?"

"My women?"

"You know what I mean."

"None of them was invited."

She didn't know whether to believe him or not, but it didn't matter. She was there with him right then, and he made her feel as if she was the only one.

"Thank you," she said.

"For what?"

"For making me feel special."

"You are special." He kissed her again. And then he tossed her into the water.

They splashed around the pool like children. After a while, he pulled himself out and grabbed a towel. "I'm going to order dinner," he said. "I'll be back."

She floated on her back, staring up at the stars. She felt as if she was having a dream, a beautiful hazy dream. When he came back outside he was wearing swim trunks and carrying a robe.

"Is the pizza already here?" she asked.

He grinned and shook his head. "I would be surprised if it arrived at all. I didn't order pizza. But if that's what you'd like…"

"No," she said, resting her arms on the side of the pool. "Whatever you ordered is fine. I like everything. Chinese…"

"How about lobster?"

"What's that dish called again?" she asked. "That one with the lobster sauce."

"No, no. I meant cooked lobsters."

"Lobster? For carryout?"

"The Four Seasons is delivering."

"The Four Seasons?" When she had been in the Bahamas before, she had wandered into the hotel, impressed by the spectacular view and surroundings. But she had nearly passed out when she saw the menu. A simple cocktail had been fifteen dollars.

She nodded toward his swim trunks and said, "Is that why you're so dressed up?"

"Exactly." He knelt close to her and said, "I'm glad you're here."

She smiled back up at him. "I am, too."

She kicked back from the edge of the pool and floated toward the middle. When she glanced back toward him, she realized that he hadn't moved. He was still kneeling at the edge of the pool, staring at her. He smiled. She swam back toward him. "What's so funny?" she asked.

"Not funny," he said. "I'm enjoying watching a beautiful mermaid swim naked in my pool."

She grinned. "If the people of Shanville could see me now, they'd never believe it."

"I'm having a hard enough time believing it myself," he said. He leaned over and kissed her.

They were interrupted by the doorbell. She gasped in horror and started to pull herself out of the pool. She had no desire to have anyone but Hunter see her naked. "Don't worry," he said. "Take your time. I'll have them set it up on the veranda."

As Hunter disappeared inside the house, Cassie wrapped the robe around her. She ran her fingers through her hair and sat down on the edge of a cushioned lounge chair. A few minutes later Hunter appeared at the door. He held out his hand to her and said, "It's ready."

The veranda was on the highest part of the property, with a sweeping view of the Atlantic. In the distance she could see the tour boats docked in the harbor, twinkling with lights.

He pulled out her chair and she sat down. He handed her a glass of champagne.

"To you," he said, sitting down and raising his glass. She took a sip.

The lobster had been cracked open, but still Cassie was unsure of how to eat it.

Hunter must have noticed because he leaned forward and stabbed a piece from the tail. He dipped it in butter and held it to her lips. She took a bite. "This is wonderful," she said, tasting the delicious, tender white meat.

They ate in silence, content to be together. It was comfortable and relaxed, as if they had been a couple for years. She felt herself wishing that they could prolong the night forever. That she would never have to leave Hunter's side.

But it was ridiculous. After all, she barely knew him. And chances were slim that their evening together would ever be repeated. A relationship was out of the question. After all, according to Hunter's father, only one woman had ever captured his heart. Cassie couldn't help but feel another twinge of jealousy as she thought of her. What had she been like? What kind of special qualities had she possessed? Before she could stop herself she said, "Your father mentioned a woman in your past."

"Sounds mysterious," he said. "What woman?"

"Your…" She hesitated. She knew she was getting into sensitive territory, and she knew it was none of her business. But she couldn't help herself. She wanted to know more about this mysterious woman. "Your fiancée," she said. She continued to chew as if she had asked him nothing more significant than the time.

"My fiancée?"

She nodded and swallowed. "Your father said you were engaged."

He shook his head. "No. I may have thought for a time that I wanted to marry her, but it was never official."

"Why not?"

He put down his fork.

She said, "You don't have to tell me if you don't want to."

"It was a long time ago," he said. "I met her when I was in college, struggling to pay the bills. We both had similar backgrounds, wanted similar things."

"You fell in love." There. She said it.

He looked at her. "I thought so."

"So what happened?"

He sighed.

"Let me guess. You became rich and famous. You changed. And she couldn't handle it."

"No. As a matter of fact, she's married to an extremely wealthy man. A man who was at one time my boss."

She glanced at him. His fiancée had married his boss?

"She broke up with me so that she could be with him," he said.

It was her turn to put down her fork.

He continued. "She told me that she could never marry a poor man."

Hunter's old girlfriend had broken his heart? "So that explains it."

"What?"

"Your drive and ambition."

"I'm not following," he said.

"Revenge."

He shook his head. "I've always been driven. And she had little effect on my ambition. But unfortunately, she did affect my relationships."

"How so?"

He shrugged. "I learned that it's impossible to really know someone."

She had to ask one more question. "What does that mean?"

"It means that for me, relationships have been at best a distraction."

He could not have inflicted more pain if he had slapped her. She was a distraction. But what did she think? Did she honestly think she would leave the Bahamas with a husband in tow? What made her think she would be any different from the rest of the women he'd slept with?

"What's wrong?" he asked.

"Nothing," she said, focusing on her empty plate. "I should thank you for your honesty. I mean, most men would lead a woman on, telling her all sorts of things she wanted to hear."

"You misunderstood." He shook his head. "I was speaking in the past tense. I thought you were looking for an explanation as to why I've never married."

She glanced up.

He stood, walked over to her and held out his hand. She accepted it, standing to face him. He said, "You're much more than a simple distraction." He cupped her face. "What about you? What happened to your marriage plans?"

She pulled away. "I don't really want to discuss that."

"Why not?"

She did not want to talk about Oliver. Not now or ever. "Because I prefer to discuss you."

"But how can I get to know you if you don't tell me more about yourself?"

She looked away. He was saying and doing all the right things. It was enough to make her believe in the future, believe that there might be a chance of a future. But how could there be?

"What's wrong?" he said. "I lost you again."

"No." She smiled sadly. "I'm just enjoying our time together."

"I am, too," he said, touching her cheek. "I am, too."

Ten

Cassie opened her eyes. Sunlight flooded the room. She was in Hunter's bedroom, a huge room with massive doors that opened to a deck.

She lay in bed as her mind replayed the wonderful scenes from the previous evening.

After dinner she and Hunter had gone back to the pool, where they had sat and held hands for what seemed like hours. Neither wanted the evening to end. Finally she had fallen asleep resting her head against Hunter's shoulder.

She awoke to him carrying her up the stairs and gently setting her down on his bed. Though half-asleep, she was still happy to realize that Hunter had brought her into his very own bedroom, his private sanctuary. He had crawled in beside her and wrapped his arms around her. They had fallen asleep with their bodies melded together.

She stretched lazily, glancing around the room for a sign of Hunter. She could hear him talking in the other room. With a burst of energy, she pulled the sheet off the bed and wrapped it around her. She followed the sound of his voice to a room down the hall. Unlike the bright, tropical tones of the other rooms, this room was done in deep, rich colors. The walls were lined with books.

Hunter stood with his back toward her. He was naked with the exception of his drawstring pajama bottoms. "Dammit!" she heard him say. She could see his back muscles flex with tension.

"I understand, Willa. But that doesn't change my mind. Had I known there was going to be a groundswell of activity, we never would've gone in there, anyway."

He turned around and smiled when he saw Cassie. His voice and appearance seemed to soften at the sight of her. "I have to go," he said into the receiver. He snapped the phone shut without saying goodbye.

He went over to Cassie and kissed her smack on the lips. "How did you sleep?"

"Great," she said. She glanced toward his phone and said, "I overheard you talking to Willa."

"I'm sorry," he said. "Not a very pleasant way to wake up."

"Is there a problem?"

"No," he said. "No problem."

He nodded toward the tray beside her. "Breakfast?" There were croissants, bagels, cream cheese and butter.

"Wow," she said. "The royal treatment."

He grasped her shoulders and said, "I was thinking…"

"What?"

"I have to attend a fund-raiser this afternoon."

Of course, she thought, her heart stopping. He wanted her to leave. Their night of passion was over. He was once again Hunter Axon, womanizer extraordinaire.

This was what she had expected, right? She should be grateful for their evening together and leave with as much dignity as possible. "That's okay," she said. "I should get going anyway.…"

"No," he said with a smile. "I'd like you to come with me."

He wanted her to stay? With him?

She found herself suddenly hesitating.

The heart that had been so wounded only seconds before suddenly filled with fear. She was already more attached than she would like. Could she handle another day...and night with him? Or would that be enough to cause her to fall hopelessly in love? "I should get back," she said quickly. "Everyone is going to be wondering what happened."

"Call them and tell them it's taking longer than you thought."

What difference could one more day make? After all, hadn't she already passed the point of no return? No matter how hard she tried, she would never forget Hunter. The damage had already been done. "Okay," she said.

He smiled. "Thank you."

"You're welcome." She kissed him and said, "Do I need a special outfit, because all I have is what you saw yesterday."

She suddenly realized that he was looking at her like a hungry lion watching its prey. "I like what you're wearing today much better," he said, moving toward her.

She pulled the sheet up around her neck as she smiled and backed up, moving toward his bedroom. "I think it's too...summery."

"Hmm," he said. He ran his hands down her sides. "I see what you mean."

"What kind of fund-raiser is this?" She was almost in the bedroom.

"A typical one. Politicians looking for rich people. Rich people looking for politicians."

"Is it supposed to benefit anyone beside rich people and politicians?"

"Children in need."

"Where is it?" Her foot hit the bed.

"It's at the racetrack," he said, gently pushing her back on the bed.

"What racetrack?"

He began unpeeling the sheet from her body. "The horse racetrack."

"The outfit I had on yesterday is dirty."

He slid his hand inside the sheet, caressing her breasts. The feeling was intoxicating. "I'll buy you a new one."

Focus. "I don't want a new one. Is there a dry cleaners on the island?" He kissed her neck.

"I think so."

"You think so?"

"I don't usually deal with laundry."

"Of course," she said sarcastically. She playfully pushed him away.

"You don't have to get hostile," he said, with a twinkle in his eye. Within a second she was flat on her back.

"Like I said," he repeated, completely removing the sheet. He took his time, his eyes seemingly drinking in every detail of her naked form. "I think the suit you have on looks just fine."

He kissed her and let go of her arms, allowing her to wrap them around his neck and hold him close.

She said, "I just can't believe that…"

"That what?"

"That I'm with you. You're so different from my expectation."

"Different good?" he asked, kissing her. "Or different bad?"

They were interrupted by his cell phone. He pushed himself up and glanced at the number. "It's my office."

"Go ahead," she said.

He sighed and swung open his phone. "Yes?"

He glanced at her. "No," he said finally. He turned away. "She spoke out of turn. Don't start yet." He closed the phone and turned back toward her. But something in his demeanor had changed.

"Is everything all right?"

"Fine," he said simply.

But she had the feeling she was not being told the whole truth. "There's not a problem, is there? A problem with Demion Mills?"

"You tell me," he said. He held a hand to her cheek. "Are you sure about this?"

She nodded.

He said, "This buy-out is going to tie you to New York…to the mill for a long, long time."

She felt her blood run cold. She knew instinctively something was wrong. Why was he trying to talk her out of her decision? "What are you getting at, Hunter?" she asked, wrapping the sheet back around her.

"I can help you, Cassie. I can help you live the life you dreamed. You could go back to school. You could pursue a career in photography."

"But I don't want a career in photography."

He was quiet for a moment. "You're saying that you're happy to spend the rest of your life just working in a factory—"

"Just?" She sat up straight. She felt as if she had been slapped.

"I'm sorry," he said quickly. "I didn't mean it that way."

"I'm proud of what I do. And I'm happy. Is it what I dreamed about as a child? No. But dreams change. So do people." She shook her head. "This may be difficult for someone like you to understand, but I'm content to be who I am. Cassie Edwards, weaver. I don't need money to make me happy."

He glanced away. "I understand that. Unfortunately, in business, money and profitability are the bottom line. It's going to take a lot more than positive thinking to turn this mill around. This would be a difficult project for the most experienced of marketing people."

"We had a deal," she said softly.

"We still do." He crossed his arms and said, "I just want you to be aware of what's in store for you. I don't want to see you get hurt."

"I'm not going to get hurt."

He walked back toward the bed and took a seat beside her. "Look. I feel like we have a future here. I'm not sure what's happening to us but I think it might be something. I'd like for us to give it a chance."

"So would I."

"Well, that's going to be difficult when I'm the one who's going to have to go in there and foreclose on your home if need be. I'm afraid this stay of execution I've given you is only temporary."

"Don't ask me to choose between you and the mill."

"I would never do that," he said. He shook his head. "Why do you think I'm willing to do this, Cassie? I care about you more than…well, more than I've cared for anyone in a long, long time. I want to help you." He stood up and walked toward the balcony. At the French doors he stared silently at the Atlantic.

The anger that was building inside Cassie suddenly dissipated. He was talking to her like a…like a friend. She walked up to him and slipped her arm around his waist.

When he turned toward her, she could see the pain in his eyes.

"I have to do this, Hunter. I will never be happy if I let my friends down."

"But you may still," he said. "The Demions couldn't make this mill work with or without the patent."

"We're not going to make the same mistakes."

"You have no experience running a company. Neither does anyone else."

"I'll learn. We'll all learn." So he thought she would fail. It was one thing to question her decision, but to insult her intelligence was another.

After all, he was wrong. Wasn't he?

Or was he?

Perhaps she was just being foolish. Perhaps the Demions had been right to sell the mill. Perhaps, even with the patent, the mill was doomed. Machines could do it faster and more accurately. So why would people be willing to pay the higher price for hand-woven garments?

But how could she stand by and do nothing?

She couldn't. For one thing was certain: the mill was worth saving.

She turned away. "I guess I'll go get ready."

He grabbed her arm and swung her around to face him. He looked sad, almost tortured. "I want you to be happy."

She had no doubt he meant it. And that single statement touched her more than all the sweet nothings she had ever heard.

She reached up and kissed him. He pulled her toward him, crushing her lips with his. Suddenly he stopped. He cradled her head in his hands, staring into her eyes. Then, as if overtaken by passion, he kissed her once again.

They came together with the desperation of a drowning man in search of air. They made love as if the connection between them was vital to their very being. It had moved beyond desire. It was now a need.

Afterward he murmured, "What have you done to me?"

She laughed and pulled herself up. "I was about to ask you the same question."

"What do you mean?"

"I've gone from virgin to…I don't know."

He kissed her.

She glanced at the clock. "What time are we supposed to leave?"

He shrugged. "An hour or so."

An hour or so? "But my clothes!"

He glanced at the heap on the floor. He opened up the bottom of his nightstand and pulled out a phonebook. He opened it up and seconds later said, "There's a one-hour dry cleaner near here." He shut the phonebook and said, "I'll take them."

"Thank you," she said, relieved. He threw on jeans and a T-shirt. He looked years younger than his age, more like a muscular surfer than a businessman.

"I'll be back," he said, holding up her clothes.

He was gone less than an hour. When he returned, she had showered and was finishing drying her hair. "Thanks again," she said, turning off the dryer and giving him a kiss. "How much time?"

He looked at his watch. "Well, considering the limousine is already here…five minutes?"

She let out a yelp, grabbed her clothes and slammed the door.

A few minutes later he was showered and changed and she was wearing the identical outfit she had worn the day before. "You look beautiful," he said.

"Thank you." She kissed him on the cheek. "But you saw this outfit yesterday."

"That doesn't change anything," he said, keeping his hands around her waist. He kissed her neck and smiled.

Then he grabbed her hand and led her out of the house.

She said, "I've never been to the horse races before."

He opened the limousine door and stopped. "I hope you're not disappointed."

She knew for a fact she would not be. How could she be disappointed as long as she was with him?

He slid in beside her and wrapped his arm around her shoulders. She snuggled against him. She was overcome by emotion. For the first time in her life she felt as if she belonged to someone. She felt loved.

He did not tell the limousine driver where he was going. Apparently the driver already knew. She turned toward Hunter and smiled. "Do you ever drive yourself?"

He laughed. "Anyplace but here."

"Why not here?"

Suddenly the limousine driver spoke. "Because I need a job." The man turned around and flashed Cassie a smile from ear to ear.

Hunter shrugged. "There you have it," he said mischievously.

Cassie laughed.

He glanced at her purse. "Got your camera?"

She smiled and patted her purse. "Naturally."

The limousine pulled into the airport. "What are we doing here?" she asked.

"We're flying to the track."

He obviously liked surprising her with transportation. A boat to a board meeting, a motorbike to lunch, a plane to the racetrack… What was next?

But if Hunter thought she was impressed by such extravagance he was wrong. She would've been just as happy traveling by foot.

He led her into a private hangar. They were greeted by an employee and led out to the tarmac where a helicopter was waiting. Hunter opened the door and assisted her inside.

"When are you going to tell me where we're going?" she asked.

"I already told you. The—"

"Racetrack. Right. I guess I should've been more specific. Where is the racetrack located?"

"It's in Florida," he said. "Outside of Miami."

The helicopter lifted off the ground, and as the vehicle surged past the Nassau skyline, she held his hand. Twenty minutes later she was looking at the coastline of Miami.

She let go of Hunter's hand and pulled out her camera. She snapped her photos as the helicopter flew past towering glass buildings. At times they were so close she could see the occupants inside.

"That's where we're going," Hunter said, pointing out the window.

She held her breath as the helicopter landed on top of a narrow building. The door suddenly opened and she was being helped out.

Hunter grabbed her hand and together they walked down the flight of stairs leading into the hotel.

"Welcome, Mr. Axon," said a man in a uniform.

They followed the man out of the hotel and into another waiting limousine. The driver nodded as they entered, but once again he did not ask them where they were going. He already knew.

They drove for another half hour to the outskirts of Miami. He pulled into a large parking lot and drove up to the entrance of the building.

Hunter took her hand. "Show time."

She followed him through the gate and over to the betting booths. She could hear the din of the crowd cheering outside in the grandstand.

Hunter picked up a betting card and glanced over it. He headed toward a booth and placed his bets. All were for one hundred dollars.

When she looked at the card, one name stood out. "Hunter," she said. She pulled out her checkbook. "I want one hundred on Hunter."

"What?" he said, fumbling for the card. He grabbed the card and shook his head. "There's a horse named Hunter?"

"Yes," said Cassie, smiling. "What are the chances of that? I think it's a sign from the heavens. That's our winning horse."

"He's a long shot," said Hunter.

"Really?" she asked.

An impeccably dressed older gentleman standing nearby joined them. "That's what they say." He shook his head. "But I'm not so sure. The more distance for this horse, the better. He's definitely a horse that gets rolling late."

"So you think he can win?" Cassie asked the man.

He shrugged his linen-encased shoulders. "As much as any other horse. You just need luck and an animal that can handle the distance."

She turned to Hunter, who looked unconvinced. "What's wrong, Hunter?" she teased. "Don't think your namesake can handle the distance?"

He shrugged. "We'll see." He reached for his wallet and told the woman in the booth, "The lady would like one hundred on Hunter."

"No way," Cassie said. "This is my bet. Don't think you're going to crash it." She nudged him out of the way. "To whom do I make the check out?"

"Don't be ridiculous," Hunter said, putting his hand over her checkbook. "I'm paying for this."

"I have a hunch," she said.

She made out the check. But before she could hand it to the woman, he stopped her. "If you put your check away," he said, "I'll wager one thousand dollars."

She smiled. "Now that's a risky bet."

"I have a hunch," he said with a grin. "Besides, didn't you just remind me this was for a good cause?"

She reluctantly put her check back in her purse, and he put down his credit card. The woman in the booth handed him a ticket, which he gave to Cassie.

They walked out to the track to see a group of horses finishing a race. "Are you hungry?" he asked Cassie. "There's a clubhouse above us." He nodded toward the glass windows overlooking the track.

She shook her head. "No," she said. He smiled and led her toward the seats near the track.

Hunter scanned the crowd and said, "I think we're sitting down there."

All of a sudden they were interrupted by a busty brunette. "Hunter? Oh, my God!"

Hunter turned. Cassie could feel him stiffen.

"I heard you were going to be here today." The woman looked at Cassie and said, "Hi."

Hunter introduced her. "Cassie Edwards, this is a friend of mine."

"Val Forbes," the woman said, giving Cassie a quick, mechanical nod. Before Cassie had a chance to respond, Val said to Hunter, "I tried to call you but your office said you were out of town."

"Yes," Hunter said. "I've been traveling."

"You look good," the woman said, her breasts heaving. "Really good." Cassie raised an eyebrow as she let go of Hunter's hand. This was no ordinary old friend. It was obvious that they had just run into one of Hunter's warm-blooded women—one whose name he hadn't recalled. Cassie could feel the warmth seep up her back. She looked the woman over carefully. Had Hunter shared his bed with her? Would he share his bed with her again?

The thought was enough to make her ill. Or at least in need of some sweets.

"Why don't you two catch up?" Cassie said. "I'll meet you at the seats."

If he wanted to talk to this beautiful woman, then let him. After all, Cassie had no claims on him. She had made a promise to herself: no commitments. Despite their intimacy, she had to force herself to keep their relationship in perspective.

She marched up to the snack booth and said, "I'd like a chocolate ice cream cone, please." She hesitated. Drastic times called for drastic measures. "Make that a double."

The man gave her the ice cream cone and Cassie began to devour it like a woman deprived.

The voice from behind her almost made her jump. "I thought you said you weren't hungry."

Cassie wiped off her chin and said, "I thought you said she was a friend."

"She is."

"Hmm. We should all have friends like that," she said, taking another lick of her ice cream.

"What's that supposed to mean?"

Her head began to pound. Cassie touched her forehead, willing the pain away.

"Are you all right?" he asked.

"Brain freeze," she said.

"Brain freeze?"

"Too much, too fast. Ice cream, that is." She held it out to him. "I'm done."

"Thanks," he said sarcastically as he accepted the half-melted cone and dumped it in the trash. "Bend over," he said.

"What?"

"I used to get brain freezes all the time when I was a kid. Bend over. I don't know how, but it works."

He massaged the back of her neck. She didn't know if it was the massage or the bend, but he was right. Her headache disappeared.

She flipped her head back up. "Much better."

He smiled. "Come on," he said, taking her hand. "Let's go sit down."

She followed him toward their seats. She wanted to ask him more questions about Val but she knew she couldn't. After all, it was none of her business. "So how do you know that woman?" she heard herself ask.

He glanced at her and said, "You're not jealous, are you?"

"Jealous?" The mere thought was laughable. She and Hunter hardly had a commitment. Besides, she knew the score.

So why was her heart burning? "Why should I be jealous?" she said as coolly as she could manage.

"No reason at all."

"I couldn't care less," she added for good measure.

"I'm glad to hear that," he said, leading her toward the two empty front-row seats. "Because it looks like we're sitting next to her."

Cassie glanced where he was pointing. There was the busty

brunette, sitting next to an even more beautiful blonde. The women had not noticed them yet. They were huddled together, as if deep in conversation. "Talk about luck!" Cassie said as enthusiastically as she could manage.

As soon as all the introductions were made once again, Cassie slid in next to the brunette. She couldn't help but notice that Hunter had let go of her hand. Was it because he didn't want to appear affectionate in front of Val?

Once they were seated, Val and the blonde continued their tête-à-tête. Cassie tried not to listen, but she was helpless to do otherwise. In only five minutes she learned more about Val than she cared to know: she just received $300 highlights, the dress she was wearing cost $800, her shoes were by Manolo Blahnik, her dinner the previous evening cost $200. The most traumatic news, the one that received an onslaught of sympathy from the blonde, was that despite having just received a $100 manicure, the nail polish on her left pinkie was already chipped.

Finally Val turned to Cassie and said, "You look familiar. Have I met you before?"

Cassie rolled her eyes. "Just minutes ago…"

"No, no," the woman laughed. "Before today."

Cassie shook her head. "I doubt it."

"At the MS benefit?"

"No."

"Was it the Governor's ball in Washington?"

"No."

"Hmm," she said. "I know I'll remember sooner or later…." She tapped her pink, slightly chipped nail on Cassie's leg. "Wait. You work for that state senator…what's his name…?"

"I work in a factory," Cassie said. Normally she did not describe the mill as a factory, but what the heck. It made a better story.

The woman laughed. "Aptly put. The state senate is a madhouse."

"No," Cassie said. "I don't work in the state senate. I'm a factory worker."

"What?" said Val, leaning forward as if she didn't hear correctly.

"I work in a factory in upstate New York."

The news had the intended effect. The women glanced at each other, stunned. Cassie could almost read what they were thinking. *Hunter Axon is dating a factory worker?*

For a moment she wondered what Hunter would feel about her revelation. Would he be embarrassed by her proclamation? That she was, as he himself had described it, just a factory worker?

But her doubts were put to rest when she felt Hunter's arm slide around her shoulders, giving her a proud squeeze.

"I don't follow," piped the blonde, leaning in. "So how did you two meet?"

"Hunter bought the factory where I work."

"Technically, honey," interrupted Hunter, "we didn't know that when we met."

Val said, "How interesting. I've never actually met a…well, someone who works in a factory before."

"Me, neither," said the blonde. "Is it as boring as it looks in the movies?"

Cassie's blood began to boil. Could these women be any more pretentious?

But she didn't have time to continue their discussion, because at that very moment, a new batch of horses took to the track.

"That's your horse," said Hunter, nodding toward the long, lean chestnut-colored one.

A shot sounded and the horses broke from the gate. Hunter the horse ripped out of the gate and rounded the first turn. "I think you have a chance," she whispered.

Hunter the horse shook off the rest of the pack one by one as he barreled into the backstretch. Cassie forgot all about the women sitting next to her. She stood up in her seat and began to holler at the top of her lungs as Hunter took the lead, flying under the wire.

Her horse had won.

Cassie screamed and threw her arms around Hunter.

He picked her up and swung her around.

"You won?" Val asked.

Cassie nodded.

"Too bad it's for charity," the blonde said. "You would've made a lot of money."

Cassie's elation turned to disdain. She turned around, facing the blonde. Was she joking? Must everything be defined by money?

"Let's go," Hunter said, pulling her out of the row before she had a chance to speak her mind. As they walked up the steps, Hunter took her arm. "Were you having fun back there, Norma Rae?"

Cassie smiled. "I don't know what you mean," she said as innocently as she could.

"I thought you forgave me for my idiotic comment earlier today."

"Which idiotic comment might that be?"

"Touché," he said with a grin. But just as quickly as it had appeared, it faded. "I was referring to the comment I made about you being a factory worker."

"I believe you said *just* a factory worker."

He pulled her to a stop. "Please forgive me," he said. His eyes looked dark and pained with guilt.

"I already have," she said, touching his cheek. But had she really? Of one thing she was sure: she had not forgotten.

As if reading her mind, he said, "I don't care what you do for a living, Cassie."

"Your friends certainly do."

"Those women aren't my friends," he said. "I'm not like them. You've met my father. You've seen where I grew up."

"I've also seen where you live."

He hesitated and said, "The plane, the boats, the big house…I could walk away from everything tomorrow. Those things don't define me."

"How do you define yourself?"

"As a fisherman. And not a very good one, either."

She had no doubt that Hunter was speaking in earnest. But could he really walk away from all of his expensive toys? From his jet-setting life? From the adoring women? She doubted it.

One thing seemed certain: her opinion mattered. He wanted her to like him. And for some reason, that realization thrilled her more than she cared to admit. "You're a lousy fisherman?"

He grinned. It was an irresistibly sexy smile that sent her pulse racing. "Worse than lousy. That's why I applied to boarding school. I knew the only chance I had to survive was to get off that island."

They turned in their winning ticket. Cassie got back a receipt that read "Thank you for your donation of one hundred thousand dollars."

One hundred thousand dollars, all to charity.

It was enough to make her want to kiss him. Without hesitating, she threw her arms around his neck and did exactly what she desired. At the moment their lips touched, a crack of thunder sounded through the stadium, followed by an announcement stating that all races were postponed.

Hunter took Cassie's hand and led her outside as the first fat raindrops began to fall. He kissed her again, harder this time. She was mildly aware of the hubbub around them. The racetrack was closing. People were closing out their bets and leaving.

He slid his hand around her waist. The wind picked up and the palm trees swayed.

The rain fell more steadily, drenching the crowd outside the track. But they did not move. They stayed there, wrapped in each other's arms, aware only of each other.

Eleven

Hunter awoke early the next morning. He lay in bed, quietly watching Cassie sleep. Most mornings he began his day with a start, jumping out of bed and hurrying off to work. But not today. When he'd woken up and felt Cassie in his arms, it was as if time had stopped. It was a feeling unlike any he had ever experienced. For the first time in his life he did not wish he were somewhere else.

Or with someone else.

But then again he had known Cassie was special from the moment they met. With each passing day, he only grew more impressed.

Like the way she had handled herself the previous day. He knew how intimidating it could be to be thrown into a crowd of snobby, wealthy socialites. But Cassie had more than held her own.

In fact, she had put those offensive women in their place. But they weren't the only ones. She had done the same with him.

Just a factory worker…

He knew how it had sounded. He didn't blame Cassie for being angry. After all, he had criticized her livelihood.

But as much as he hated to admit it, a part of him assumed she could do better. That an intelligent, gifted woman such as she could not be happy working for minimum wage and making fabric.

There was no way around it. Cassie was right. He was behaving like an elitist.

And she was right to be offended. After all, what was wrong with working in a factory? Or, in this case, an old mill? Maybe it was not as lucrative as a corporate job, but then again, it didn't have the headaches, either. Cassie made a decent living at an honorable profession.

More important, Cassie worked with people she loved and trusted. And at the end of the day, she went home with the knowledge that she had helped to create something beautiful.

How many people could say that about their jobs?

Certainly not him.

Axon Enterprises was a profit-making machine, a corporate behemoth that cared little for humanity. Money was the bottom line, the definition of success. And ethics were nonexistent.

He would be the first to admit that the path he had chosen was a difficult one. With the exception of his father and a handful of others he had known from childhood, he trusted no one. He had learned firsthand that money did not buy happiness. He had a house he barely lived in, a boat he never used. He had grown accustomed to a life devoid of meaning.

But he had never been aware of it as much as he was right then and there.

He had wanted to prove to Cassie that he was not the cold, ruthless man she imagined. But perhaps she was right. After all, what kind of man was willing to make a living off other people's failures? What kind of man could displace workers who had worked at a factory for generations?

He shook off the covers and swung his feet to the floor.

He sat on the edge of the bed and put his head in his hands. What was he doing? Why was he suddenly so anxious to prove the morality of what he did?

Cassie.

He sat up straight and looked at her once again. She had not moved. Her beauty was intense, almost ethereal. She had the face of an angel, thick, black lashes, dusty-rose cheeks and a smooth, ivory complexion.

What was she doing to him?

Being with Cassie had forced him to deal with all the issues he had denied for too long.

Her power over him was as strong as it was undeniable. Cassie inspired him to be a better man.

But how could that be? He barely knew her.

But it didn't seem to matter. He had to help her.

He knew that in spite of her protestations, she did not fully realize how difficult it would be to increase the mill's revenues. Demion Mills produced only two to twenty yards of fabric a day. Computerized looms made twenty to one hundred yards a day.

And the machines in the mill were old; most original. The newer machines did the work of six iron-and-wood looms. He knew the Demions had borrowed heavily against the mill just to make payroll. Most of the mills like Demion had shut down, moving operations to the Far East, or replacing people with computers.

But what if Demion Mills was the sole producer of Bodyguard?

He had not agreed to sell them the patent, but was the mill worth anything without it?

And could the patent alone save the mill?

Probably not. Oliver Demion had realized this. When he found that the material his family had been producing for use in lawn chairs was suitable as an absorbent undergarment for athletes, he had done the most intelligent thing he could think of: sell it along with the mill. Oliver knew the patent was worth a small fortune, and the mill, even if it was capable of producing it, had no money to commit to marketing efforts.

But the mill needed that patent. Without it Cassie and her friends could never hope to stay in business. Within a year the mill would be hemorrhaging money. In two years it would be closed.

But the introduction of Bodyguard would require a substantial sum of money. An amount Demion Mills did not have.

So what should he do? What could he do?

"What are you thinking about?" Cassie asked, blinking her eyes sleepily. Her beautiful auburn hair was splayed over the white pillowcase.

"You," he said.

She reached out her hand and touched his cheek, smiled. She nodded toward his watch. "What time is it?"

"Nearly nine."

She sat up straight. "I should get back to Shanville."

He nodded. "I'm going with you."

"To Shanville?"

"Yes. I want to talk to some of the artisans and get a feel for your production capabilities."

"Oh. Okay. Why?"

"Because…" He stumbled. He did not want to tell her he was considering giving her back the patent until he was sure the mill could handle the production. "There are some things I need to take care of to get ready for the transfer."

She removed her hand. "You're not having second thoughts again, are you?" she asked.

Second thoughts? Was it possible that she still did not trust him? He pushed himself up on one arm. "No. I'm selling you the mill. But it's still complicated." He leaned over her. "I don't want you to fail."

"You don't need to worry," she said. "We're using our homes as leverage, remember?"

"So I should be content with the knowledge that I will be foreclosing on everyone's homes? That I would essentially own a town?"

She hesitated. He saw a flicker of apprehension cross her face. "You would rather have your money," she said, as if stating a fact. He saw the disappointment in her eyes.

She was wrong. It was not about money. At least, not this time. But he did not tell her that. He needed to prove that he could behave honorably. He needed her to trust him.

He kissed her shoulder. "Get dressed," he said quietly. "We have work to do."

Cassie stood on the factory floor. She looked around her. It had been a three-hour flight back to Shanville, yet she felt as if she were worlds away. The sleek glamour of Hunter's Bahamian world was nowhere to be seen. Instead it was as if she had been transported back through time. Heavy, Victorian-era machinery was packed into the large room. She closed her eyes and listened to the familiar thwack of silk threads being beaten back by wood battens, a sound so musical her grandmother had written a poem about it as a child.

All around her were friends, women she had known her entire life. They worked the clattering looms, nimble fingers flying over the taut ropes, cast-iron flywheels.

Cassie had told her co-workers that their offer had been accepted. But instead of joy and jubilation, it was a quiet peace. Everyone knew that they may have won the battle, but that did not mean they were going to win the war.

"Cassie." She felt a warm pat on her arm. Luanne said, "You did good. And we're all grateful." Luanne handed Cassie a small card to tuck into the loom. Cardboard cards, each punched with holes to determine the ornate patterns in the weave, were kept on long strings looped over the looms. A complex pattern might require as many as 20,000 cards. The system was developed in the eighteenth century and still used.

"Luanne's right," Ruby said. "You saved our mill all by yourself. Your grandma would be proud."

Luanne shook her head. "And she'd be happy that you're through with Oliver after what he did to us all."

"We have the mill back again. The past is the past," Cassie said.

"But we don't have the patent," Luanne said.

"No," Cassie admitted. And they never would. Hunter might

finance a loan for the mill, but the patent was too valuable. He would never agree to sell it for what they could offer.

Luanne sighed and shrugged her shoulders. "I guess Oliver did what he had to do. Can't blame a man for wanting to make money."

"Why not?" said Priscilla. She, too, had worked in the mill all her adult life. "Why can't you blame him?"

Cassie understood their anger. But she no longer felt anything toward Oliver one way or the other. Her mind had been taken over by Hunter. All she could think about was Hunter—what he had said, what he had done. How he had touched her. How they had kissed.

She felt as if he possessed not only her body but her soul as well.

And that troubled her.

In a way, she wished she'd never seen the man behind the image. That she'd never heard about the poor boy who had learned early on that money was a ticket to survival. That she had never heard about his grandmother's death and the brutal loss of the woman he loved.

But learning how he had come to be a corporate raider was not the same as accepting it. Money was his crutch, his way of self-protection. But his motives could not be glorified. Nor could they be excused.

She knew it was useless to think that perhaps she had a chance to convince him otherwise.

Or could she?

After all, it was obvious that he wanted to help her. Didn't he? And that was commendable.

The truth of the matter was she wanted to give him a chance. The man she had spent time with was capable of extreme caring and kindness. She was sure of it.

Wasn't she?

Could the man who had held her in his arms and stared into her eyes while making love to her take her house out from under her?

Yet hadn't he threatened to do just that? *So I should be content with the knowledge that I will be foreclosing on everyone's homes?*

The problem was, she realized, that she was already confusing business with pleasure. And she doubted Hunter would make the same mistake.

After all, he had seemed so cold and distant on the flight back. He had barely spoken with her, choosing instead to work on his computer. She had felt self-conscious and awkward. With nothing to do, she had busied herself by fiddling with her camera and taking the occasional picture.

"I don't understand why he's still here," Priscilla continued.

"Who?"

"Hunter Axon."

Cassie blushed at the mention of her lover's name. She still had not told anyone of their affair. "He wanted to talk to some of us about production," she said.

"But," Priscilla continued, "why should it matter, if he's selling us the mill?"

"Because he's financing it," Luanne said.

"He doesn't want to sell us back the mill only to see it fail," Cassie said. "If we don't succeed, he's not going to get any money."

"Is that it? Or does he have a more personal investment in our success?"

Cassie could not answer her old friend. How could she explain that she had fallen in love with the man they considered an enemy?

Priscilla put a hand on hers, stopping the loom.

Cassie looked at her, her eyes full of torment.

Priscilla smiled kindly and said, "Is he worried that you'll end up getting hurt?"

"He's a decent man…he is. I know you've all seen a side to him that's…well, less than flattering but…"

"We all know that, Cassie. He's giving us back our mill."

Luanne grinned and said, "I couldn't be happier for you. After Oliver, I was hoping that you might meet someone else soon. And who could you possibly meet around here?" She rolled her eyes in emphasis.

Cassie glanced around the room. The women were all nodding their heads supportively. Cassie smiled in appreciation and said, somewhat meekly, "I didn't mean for this to happen." Cassie slid in another card. "I doubt this...whatever it is between Hunter and me, will turn into anything." She sighed. "I'm sorry. I hope I haven't complicated things. I never should've gotten involved with him in the first place."

"He's back here, isn't he?" Luanne said. "He obviously cares."

Cassie hesitated. More than anything, she wanted to believe that Hunter cared about her.

"If I were you, I'd give him a chance. He's an important, busy man. And he's trying to help us. That's something."

Luanne was right. He had come back.

There was hope. There was definitely hope.

"You're not serious." Willa fixed her gaze on Hunter as she tapped her long, manicured nails on the wooden table in her makeshift office.

Hunter had just finished telling Willa of his plans. "I am."

"Do you have any idea how many hours I've spent on this project? How much time I've spent securing this deal?"

"You will be compensated, Willa. As usual."

"This is not a typical deal for me."

"I understand that."

"Oliver was counting on us moving production to the Far East."

"Oliver will receive the compensation he was promised."

"Don't be foolish, Hunter. You could lose millions."

Hunter appreciated Willa's concern, but she was not telling him anything he did not already know. He had little choice. He could not leave Cassie in Shanville with a mill that was headed for bankruptcy. "You're forgetting that with the deal I have in mind, I would still retain a percentage of the fees gained from the patent."

"That patent is worthless unless they know how to market it."

"So we will help them."

"Why not just do it ourselves? Why share the rights?" She shook her head.

"There's more at stake than money. These people…well, they've invested their entire lives in this mill."

"So what?" She shrugged. "That's never stopped you before."

What could he say? Willa was right. He'd never really cared before. But he did now. The people of Shanville were no longer anonymous small-town workers. How could he tell himself that taking over the mill was in their best interests, when he knew otherwise? He continued, "Instead of the Far East you will return to the Bahamas."

"Hunter, please. This is all that factory worker's doing."

He did not need to ask to whom she was referring. He felt a sting of tension in the back of his neck. How dare Willa refer to Cassie with that snobbish tone? "She's not a factory worker," he said. "She's a weaver who's trying to save her mill."

"This has nothing to do with saving a mill. This is about revenge. Plain and simple."

"Revenge?"

Willa was silent for a moment. "You don't know?"

"Know what?"

"Cassie and Oliver were engaged."

Hunter hesitated. It wasn't possible. Cassie and…Oliver? The man from whom he bought the mill? The man who followed Willa around like a devoted puppy? "Oliver Demion?" he heard himself say.

"Apparently she had been in love with him since she was a child. But he never really loved her. He got engaged because he felt obligated. They had been together since they were kids."

Hunter was silent. Why hadn't Cassie told him that Oliver had been her fiancé?

"But once he met me, he knew he had to break things off with Cassie. She was devastated." Willa shook her head and sighed. "Poor Oliver. He felt so guilty." She shrugged. "In any case, he felt guilty until Cassie swore revenge."

Hunter couldn't believe what he was hearing. It couldn't be true. Cassie was interested in revenge?

"Oliver predicted she would set her sights on you. But I give her credit. I never thought you'd actually fall for it. And I certainly never thought she'd be able to persuade you to sell the company."

That was it. Hunter had heard enough.

"I don't have time for idle gossip, Willa, and neither do you."

With that he left the room. He walked down the hall toward his office. Had he misjudged Cassie? Had she been playing him all along just to get what she wanted?

Had he missed the cues? Was he just a pawn?

After all, it had happened before. He'd thought he'd known Lisa. Apparently he hadn't known her at all. Everyone had seen her for who she really was but him. He had been blinded by love.

He'd sworn it would never happen again. After all, he had been a boy when he was with Lisa. He had been with many women since. He thought he could tell the good from the bad. He thought he could recognize the diamond from the rhinestones.

But perhaps he had given himself too much credit. Perhaps Willa was right. Perhaps Cassie was only using him to win back an old love.

Did it matter?

Hell, yes.

He could feel himself close up, feel his heart freeze once again. He had given too much too soon. And he had no choice but to pay the price.

But what could he do?

He cared about her too much to walk away and leave her with an old mill destined for failure.

No.

He would do the honorable thing. He would give Cassie the mill and the patent.

But then he was through. His relationship with Cassie would be defined solely through business.

If it was revenge she was after, she would have to obtain it alone.

Twelve

Cassie stared at the phone. It was nearly nine o'clock at night, well past the dinner hour. Hunter hadn't called. And it was becoming more and more obvious that he had no intention of calling.

So what did that mean? Was he just busy? Or, she thought, her heart sinking, had he reached a decision regarding the mill that he knew she would not like?

What decision might that be, however? He had told her he would sell her the mill. She believed him. He would not renege.

So what was it, then? Why hadn't he called her?

She had heard he was leaving the next day and was spending the night at a hotel in town. She'd assumed he had booked the hotel room for the sake of appearances. It had never occurred to her he actually planned on sleeping there. Alone.

She swallowed. Perhaps his reason for not calling was a more personal one.

Cassie stood up and walked toward the window. A cold and bitter wind rattled the panes, seeping through the cracks. Despite her wool cardigan, Cassie shivered. She crossed her arms in an attempt to ward off the chill.

It was hard to believe that only the night before she had slept naked, enjoying the warm breeze from the open French doors. It was equally hard to believe that the man with whom she had shared a bed, the man who had made some passionate and tender love, was no longer interested in her.

But it was a scenario she had to consider.

In rapid progression, she imagined the worst. Perhaps he thought their differences too numerous. Perhaps he had grown tired of her. Perhaps he never really cared. Perhaps…their relationship was over.

If it was over, she should not be surprised. After all, they had become intimate very early in their relationship. She had known it was risky. She had known she was setting herself up for rejection, known that their relationship would end eventually. Hadn't she?

Maybe. But a part of her had hoped for a miracle. A part of her had actually believed that Hunter cared. That their lovemaking was every bit as special to him as it was to her.

Was she wrong?

It seemed difficult to believe that he suddenly had a change of heart. Yet from the moment they left the Bahamas she had sensed a difference. It was subtle, but still noticeable. A slight stiffening. A pulling away.

But would he leave town without so much as a goodbye?

Cassie turned away from the window. What was wrong with her? Why was she analyzing everything like the soon-to-be-jilted lover? Perhaps the reason he hadn't called was something less dramatic. Perhaps he was just distracted by work.

Or perhaps not. Perhaps he had no intention of calling her now or ever again.

She glanced once again at the phone. She checked her watch. She knew where he was staying. And if he had tired of her or was ready to break up with her, she wanted to hear it in person.

* * *

Hunter took off his watch and set it on the night table. He undid his cuff links and began unbuttoning his shirt. His mind, as it had been all day, was focused on Cassie.

He had spent the afternoon and evening holed up in an empty office, busying himself with work in an attempt to distract himself from the pain in his heart. But it had been in vain.

Damn!

How could he have been so naive?

He didn't want to believe that their relationship was based on revenge, yet the facts proved otherwise. Why else had she not told him the truth about who her fiancé was? Why was she so willing to give up her dream of a career in photography just to save the mill? Why did she lose her virginity to a stranger?

She had been motivated by love.

A love not for him, but for someone else.

He was interrupted from his reverie by a knock on the door. He was in no mood for distractions nor company. "Come in," he barked.

Cassie opened the door.

The mere sight of her was enough to take his breath away. But he could not give in to his body. He needed to control his feelings. He needed to focus. To concentrate. He turned away and continued unbuttoning his shirt. "What are you doing here?"

He could hear her shut the door.

"What's going on?" she asked quietly.

"What do you mean?"

"The way you just greeted me. Something is wrong, isn't it?"

"I'm tired, Cassie. It's not every day I give a company back."

"Is that it?" she asked, shutting the door. "Are you having second thoughts?"

"Would it matter?" he asked.

She glanced down.

"No," he said. "I didn't think so."

"So this is about money?"

"Why don't you tell me," Hunter said, facing her.

"What are you talking about?"

"As I mentioned to you before, everything usually boils down to money," he said, taking a step toward her.

She lifted her head, defiant. "Maybe with you."

"But not with you?" he said. He stood in front of her. He could see the outline of her firm breasts underneath her snug jacket. Her jeans seemed to wrap around her slender hips.

"No," she said. "I don't think money is all that important in the scheme of things."

He could feel himself weaken. Damn, she was beautiful. "Tell me," he said, "if money doesn't motivate you, what does?"

"What do you mean?"

He took a step toward her. "Why are you so desperate to keep the mill?"

"I told you. This mill is in our blood. It's who we are. Some of the people who work here have worked here their whole lives. They can't just pick up and move on."

"But you could. Right?"

"We've been over this," she said impatiently. "This is not about me."

"So there's no…personal reason for wanting the mill back."

"Of course. I love the mill, I love making fabric."

"And Oliver? Do you love him, as well?"

She swallowed.

He could see a change come over Cassie at the reference to Oliver. A flash of grief tore through him. So it was true. "Why didn't you tell me?"

She said, "I wasn't trying to keep Oliver's identity a secret. I would've told you about him if I thought it important. But he didn't have anything to do with us or what I wanted."

"You and Oliver were childhood sweethearts?"

"Yes." She shrugged. "Everyone just assumed that we would get married, including me."

He felt as if his heart was twisted in two. He hated this feeling of insecurity. Of uncertainty. "The breakup must have been painful for you," he said stiffly.

"Not for the reasons you might think. It was more difficult to find out that the person I thought I had loved no longer existed. I missed who he used to be, the friendship we once shared. But even still, I knew that he had done us both a favor. There was no passion in our relationship."

No passion? Was it true? Was her virginity due to a lack of physical chemistry?

He wanted to believe her. He wanted to think that the reason she gave him such a precious gift was because of their connection—the spark between them. Not because she was trying to erase another man's touch.

Cassie had not expected to be greeted by a barrage of questions regarding Oliver.

What was happening? Why was he so upset about her not telling him the name of her fiancé?

Hunter turned away from her and continued to unbutton his shirt.

She said, "Hunter…I'm sorry. Is that what's bothering you? The fact that I was engaged to Oliver?"

He turned back toward her. His eyes were dark and dangerous. "Of course not. Why would I care about your past romantic history?"

If he meant to injure her, he had succeeded. Why would he care? Because she wanted him to care. She wanted him to love her.

"My concerns are business related," he said coldly. "I don't want Axon Enterprises to get involved in a simple domestic dispute."

A domestic dispute? "Do you think I'm trying to buy the mill back just to spite Oliver?"

"Are you?"

She paused for a moment, speechless. How could he even think her capable of such a spiteful act? Did he really think that she would have risked losing her friends' severance just so she could exact revenge?

Yes.

She could tell from the way he was acting that he not only thought that, he was convinced. He had made up his mind. And nothing she said would make any difference. To argue otherwise would only make her appear defensive.

Her heart sank.

Why hadn't she told him about Oliver sooner? Didn't she realize that he would find out sooner or later the name of her ex-fiancé?

"Hunter," she said, making a move toward him.

He stepped away from her. It was a slight change, a shift in weight. But the message was clear. He did not want her near him.

What could she do to change his mind? What could she say? Nothing. The damage was done.

She glanced away and reached for the doorknob. "I made a mistake coming here. I'm sorry I bothered you."

Before she could leave, he grabbed her arm and pulled her to him. He stared into her eyes as if searching for something. "You didn't answer my question. Are you buying the mill out of spite?"

"No." She looked into his eyes. They were dark and angry, devoid of feeling.

She had spent the past few days loving him. But it was over. The realization was like an arrow through her heart.

"Why did you come here tonight?" he asked.

"I came here to see you," she said. "I couldn't stand the thought of you still being in town and not being with me."

Hunter let go of her and turned away. But not fast enough. She had seen something in his eyes. A softening. A glimmer of hope.

Suddenly it hit her like a bolt from the blue. He was jealous of Oliver.

Was it possible?

How could he be jealous of a man she never truly desired? Although she hadn't mentioned Oliver by name, she had spoken about the lack of passion in their relationship. Wasn't her virginity proof? She said, "I was never in love with Oliver. Never. I cared about him as a sister cares about a brother."

He turned back to face her. "Yet you were willing to marry him."

She sighed. "We got engaged while still in high school. He was different then. When we were growing up he was my best friend. I never thought he would end up being so deceitful. So motivated by money." She sighed. "In retrospect, I should've broken it off a long time ago, but—" she shrugged "—I don't think I would actually have gone through with it."

She stepped toward him again. "I'm sorry I didn't tell you about him," she said. "But the time with you was so special to me…so magical." She hesitated. "I didn't want to tarnish it by talking about Oliver."

He was looking at her as if deciding what to do with her. She glanced away and asked, "Do you want me to leave?"

She held her breath as she waited for the response.

He shook his head. "No," he said. She turned back toward him. His eyes lightened before her, becoming tender and kind once again.

She touched his bare chest as she breathed in the deep, musky scent of his aftershave. She would prove to him how she felt. How much she cared.

He did not touch her. Instead he turned his head ever so slightly and said hoarsely, "What are you doing to me?"

She was not ready to give up. She leaned forward and kissed him. It was like throwing a match on an oil spill. Flames ignited as he pulled her to him, kissing her mouth, her eyes, her cheeks. She reached inside his shirt, running her fingers down his bare torso.

He inhaled sharply as she made her way to the edge of his pants, tucking her fingers inside.

He pulled her hands away, and she looked at him. Why was he stopping her?

He met her gaze and said, "I want to see you."

"What?" she asked.

"I want to see you. All of you."

"You want me to take my clothes off?" She glanced toward the bathroom and said, "Okay. I'll be right back."

"No," he said, shaking his head as he pulled her back toward him. "Here." He was speaking matter-of-factly, as if giving instructions to an employee. "I want to watch you."

He wanted to…watch?

She felt a flutter of nerves. Like a striptease?

The thought was enough to bring a blush to her cheeks.

But why should she be embarrassed? After all, he had seen her naked before.

He was watching her carefully. Was this some sort of test? Whatever it was, she was up for it. Without answering him, she kicked off her shoes and socks. She stood before him and met his gaze directly, silently accepting his dare. Slowly she unzipped her pants, taking her time wiggling out of them.

His eyes darkened and his breath grew ragged as she pulled her turtleneck over her head and dropped it to the floor. Left with nothing but her bra and panties, she paused. She stood before him, teasing him with time. She unhooked her bra and tossed it on the bed. She stuck her thumbs into her panties and slowly pulled them off.

She knew he half expected her to get naked and jump under the covers, but she was emboldened by the heightened sense of passion. She could see the effect she was having on him. After a day of waiting for him to contact her, she was back in control.

And she was not ready to hand over the reins. She stood there, staring at him as his breath grew ragged. "What next?" she asked.

He held out his hand. When she took it, he yanked her on the bed, on top of him. Suddenly he was inside her, moving deeper and deeper.

They made love staring into each other's eyes, not even looking away when tension became unbearable and release necessary.

When he pulled her close to him afterward and tucked her inside the covers, she wrapped her arms around him. "I wish we could stay like this always," she said.

But Hunter did not answer. Instead, feigning sleep, he removed his arm and turned away from her.

Hours later Cassie was still awake.

Why hadn't he answered her? Why had he turned away?

She knew the answer without asking. It was as simple as it was undeniable: Hunter did not share her sentiment.

How could she have thought that Hunter was jealous of Oliver? The truth of the matter was that Hunter had been distant from the moment they set foot on the plane to return to Shanville, before he found out about Oliver. Oliver had just been a convenient excuse for him to escape.

She guessed that the real reason for Hunter's emotional distance was that their relationship had progressed too far too fast. And her coming to his hotel room had not helped matters.

But if he wasn't interested in her, how could he have made love to her?

Because he was a man. Sex and love were completely different things.

She felt like a fool. Why couldn't she just play it cool? Why did she have to act so...so desperate?

The truth of the matter was their relationship had been doomed from the night they met, the night they first made love. Her grandmother had warned her that making love changes things between a man and a woman. It was, she had said, the most intimate of connections, a connection that for some women, could never be undone.

Cassie had commended herself on refraining from premarital sex, but as she had admitted to Hunter, the wait had not been difficult. She had not been possessed by the instinctual, overwhelming desire she felt for Hunter.

And now that she had experienced such passion, her life was forever changed. For the rest of her life she would feel a bond with Hunter. And what kind of bond, if any, would he feel for her?

None. She would become another notch on his belt. Just another nameless woman with whom he had shared his bed.

She gingerly pushed the covers away and slipped out of bed. Moving in the dark, she found her clothes and put them back on. She stopped and paused, looking at him. It was time to say goodbye.

But as she turned away, he caught her in an iron grip. "Where are you going?"

"Home," she said, startled.

"Why?" he asked.

"I just…well, I should be getting back," she said. *Play it cool.* "I have to get up early tomorrow and I don't have my clothes here."

He let go of her arm and pushed himself up in bed. If she had been expecting a protest, she would've been disappointed. "Okay," he said.

All right, then. They were in agreement. She just needed to pick up her purse and walk out. Before she started crying.

"Wait," he said. He threw back the covers and turned on the light. "I'll see you home."

As he jumped out of bed, she watched his sinewy body tug on his boxers.

"No," she said quickly. "Go back to sleep. It's late."

"Did you drive here?" he asked, ignoring her protest.

"Really," she said, grabbing her coat. "I'll just be on my way. I'll talk to you tomorrow." She realized with horror that she sounded as if she was expecting him to call. "Or, um, whenever."

She opened the door but he was too quick. He shut it with his foot as he put on his coat. "Did you drive?" he repeated.

She gave up. He was too stubborn to be talked out of this. Even though it made no sense, no sense at all.

"This is ridiculous," she said. "What are you going to do? Follow me in your car?"

"My rental's already been returned. I'll drop you off and drive your car back. I'll see that it gets back to you."

Meaning he was not planning on spending the remainder of the night with her. In fact, he was willing to go to a lot of trouble to ensure that he did not have to sleep with her again.

He had his hand on the door when she touched his arm, stopping him. "Why are you doing this?"

"I'm not about to let you go home by yourself in the middle of the night."

"It's Shanville. It's perfectly safe."

He opened the door. "Let's go."

Thirteen

This was not the first time he had seen a date home after making love. He preferred it to spending the whole night together. He found the act of physically sleeping with someone even more intimate than intercourse.

But usually he didn't end up in this predicament. He rarely invited a woman into his own bed. He liked being able to leave when he wanted to.

It was just one of the ways he had managed to keep things simple. He had avoided heartbreaks by avoiding the pitfalls that encouraged a relationship.

But it was never much of a problem. Typically he was attracted to the very women who would welcome a casual liaison. Women who had little desire for a more permanent relationship. If, for some reason, things changed, he was quick to recognize the signs. Usually when a woman wanted him to meet her family he had one foot out the door already. For he had a simple rule—any mention of family meant he had taken the relationship one step too far. He did not want to meet the mother who "would absolutely love him" or the grandfather who "would never believe his granddaughter was dating a millionaire." Family only complicated things.

He always tried to be honest. He never promised a connection, a special relationship. Until now. And look what he had done. He had almost made a mistake. Or had he?

Cassie had claimed that she no longer felt anything for Oliver. That her need for the mill, her need for him, was not based on revenge.

But he was having a difficult time believing her. Not that he didn't want to. After all, he had hoped things might be different with Cassie. He wanted them to get to know each other. His usual rules regarding relationships and commitment had not applied.

He had made an exception and it had almost cost him.

As they walked outside, they were hit with a blast of cold air. The wind had died down and the night was eerily silent. Their footsteps echoed through the deserted parking lot as they made their way toward an old green Ford LTD.

"This is it," Cassie said, nodding toward the car. "The official grandparent mobile. Complete with a box of tissues in the back window."

"I'll drive," he said.

Cassie tossed him the keys. He caught them in his gloved hand and unlocked the door. Once they were settled, Hunter turned the ignition and…nothing.

She said, "Sometimes you have to turn it a couple of times. I think it might need a checkup."

Finally the engine roared to life. As usual, the car began to rattle and shake.

"I'm not an expert on cars," Hunter said, "but I think this one definitely needs some engine work."

She said, "The nearest car repair is a half hour away. And it's expensive."

"I'll take care of it for you."

"No," she said, mortified. Why had she said the part about it being expensive? And why, when it was obvious he wanted nothing more to do with her, would he volunteer to fix her car? "I don't want you to take care of it for me."

"Why not?"

"Because," she said. "I can take care of it myself."

They drove for a while. A heavy, awkward silence filled the car. Cassie was overwhelmed by a feeling of loss. How had this happened? How could they be so intimate yet so distant?

He pulled into the driveway and stopped. Once again it was time for goodbye. "Thank you," she said.

It was her eyes. They looked almost luminous in the moonlight. Open and trusting...and hurt. He could not go back to the hotel. Not without her.

He turned off the car and offered her the keys. "Aren't you leaving?" she asked.

"That's up to you."

"Hunter, I don't want you to stay because you feel pressured or something."

"Pressured?"

"I know you're trying to be honorable, but I didn't intend for this to be an all-nighter."

Had he misread her? Had his narcissistic mind been so busy focusing on his own reticence that he hadn't noticed that perhaps she wanted nothing more from him? Perhaps Willa had been wrong. Perhaps Cassie was not looking for revenge. Perhaps she was looking for some fun, a connection with another man. Perhaps loneliness had been her only motivation. "You were looking for sex?"

He could see her recoil at his harsh words. Right away, he cursed himself for insulting her. What was wrong with him? "I'm sorry. I just meant—"

"Is that what you're looking for?" she interrupted. "Sex?"

Something about the way she said it melted his heart. "No," he said. He pushed a tendril of hair away from her face. "No," he repeated, even more adamantly.

She glanced away.

He knew then why Cassie had insisted on going home. She had wanted to leave the warm comfort of his hotel room simply because she felt it was what he wanted.

He had heard her, of course, when she'd said she wished they could remain in each other's arms. But as much as he longed for the very same thing, he had been unable to respond. The news about Oliver had thrown him. He wanted to believe that Cassie was not using him, but he couldn't ignore the facts. Still, he didn't like to think that he'd somehow made Cassie uncomfortable. *"Je suis desolé,"* he murmured.

"What does that mean?"

He suddenly realized he had spoken to her in French. As a child he would lapse into French in moments of duress, usually when speaking to his grandmother. "It means I'm sorry."

She hesitated, allowing his words to sink in. Finally she said, "What did you say to me that day on the cliff?"

He said, *"Tu es la femme la plus belle que j'ai jamais vu.* You are the most beautiful woman I have ever seen."

"I had a feeling it didn't have to do with the weather." She smiled. "Thank you." She blushed slightly and glanced out the window. He had made her nervous. She tapped her hands against her knees and said, "Did you know the founder of the mill was French? William Demion?"

Hunter shook his head.

"He emigrated from France in the early nineteen hundreds. He headed toward Shanville because he'd heard that there was plenty of work mining slate. But when he arrived, he saw a truckload of looms headed for the dump and offered the driver ten dollars for the lot."

"I take it he never mined slate."

She shook her head. "The driver of the truck turned out to be the weaver. He hired him, and Demion Mills was born."

He glanced away. He did not want to discuss Demion Mills. Nor did he want to discuss her ex-fiancé's ancestor.

"Do you feel like going for a walk?" she asked.

"A walk? It's almost midnight."

"There's something I want to show you."

"Sure," he said. After all, he was leaving for France the next day. And as much as he wanted to see Cassie again, would he?

When they stepped outside, she held out her hand. "Come on," she said.

He followed her through the cold, moonlit night. Scattered remnants of the winter's hard snow crunched under their feet as they headed toward the woods. The full moon lit the path. "It's strange, isn't it?" she said. "I mean, just two nights ago we were swimming in the buff. And here we are tromping through the snow."

As they walked out of the clearing, she paused. They were standing at the top of a hill. "This is my view at the top of the world."

The town of Shanville was lit below them. They could see the railroad tracks and the factory. He could even see his hotel.

She continued, "I started coming here right after my parents passed away. I figured it was the highest spot around, so it made me closer to heaven."

He pulled her close. "What happened to them?"

"They were in a car accident when I was five. My grandparents raised me."

"Did your parents both work at Demion Mills?"

"Yep. They met in college. When they graduated, my mother wanted to move back to Shanville. The mill was the only place they could find work."

He touched her cheek, as if brushing away an invisible tear. "What college did they go to?"

"Michigan State." She turned toward him. "I went to the same school myself…until my grandmother got sick."

"That's where you studied photography?"

"Yes."

He swallowed. As much as he hated to admit it, he wanted to ask about Oliver. "It must have been difficult being so far away from Oliver."

"No," she said without hesitation. She met his eyes and said, "I guess that should have been a clue that things were not right, but I just assumed it was because we were so secure in our relationship."

She hesitated and said, "I can't really explain why Oliver and I stayed together so long. All I can think was that, since I'd known him my whole life, our relationship was all I knew." She sighed. "But now that I've met you, I'm not so sure that I ever loved Oliver. Maybe it was just friendship. I know one thing for certain. I don't love who he has become. I never thought he could do this."

"Do this?"

"Destroy the mill. Then sell what was left to someone who… well…" She hesitated.

"Planned to close it down."

"It's in his blood, just like the rest of us. He grew up here."

"I wouldn't demonize him for his choice, Cassie. From what I can see, turning the mill's fortunes around at this point is not easy." What was he doing? Defending her ex-fiancé?

"It was his responsibility," she said, without hesitation.

Hunter could tell by the tone of her voice that Cassie felt betrayed and angry at Oliver's decision to sell the mill. But was there more to it than that? Would she still be angry if they were together? If Oliver had not left her for another woman?

She took his hand and held it. They stood there for a while, neither speaking as they stared back over the town. Finally she tugged on his hand and said, "Come on."

But she did not lead him back to the house. Instead they went down the ravine, walking in the opposite direction..

He knew where Cassie was taking him next. "Are we going to the mill?"

She nodded. "I want to show you something."

"Do you have a key on you?" he asked.

She shook her head. "We don't need a key."

They made their way through the ravine and back up the other side. He followed her down a moonlit path that led to the street. The mill was directly across from them.

Cassie said, "Wait here."

"I'm not going to let you walk around in the dark by yourself," he said.

"Why not? I've done this a million times. Besides, I don't want to give away my secret."

"What secret?" he asked.

She laughed as she led him around the side of the mill to the old cellar entrance. She yanked on the rusty lock.

"Breaking and entering?" he asked.

She smiled as the lock popped open. "Call the police."

He helped her open the door and followed her down the musty old steps. "Do many people know about your secret entrance?"

"Just me." She turned on a light. They were in an old, brick-lined basement. They were surrounded by stacks and stacks of old newspapers.

"These belonged to the original owner," she said, pointing to the papers. "He kept all the papers that had anything to do with the mill. Just piled them up in the basement. No one's ever moved them."

He followed her up a flight of rickety stairs that led to the main floor. She flicked on the lights. In front of her was the unofficial photo gallery, a series of framed pictures detailing the mill's history and its proudest achievements.

Hunter had walked past these pictures many times, but he had never really looked at them.

"That was the official presidential chair used in the Carter administration," Cassie said. He moved closer for a better look at the picture to which Cassie pointed. Two women stood behind a beautiful chair, smiling proudly.

She continued, "The young woman standing directly behind the chair is my mother. My grandmother is standing to her right. They made that material. Tuscan Vine Demion silk lampas. One thousand dollars a yard."

The women, like Cassie, had auburn hair and sharp green eyes. They looked more like sisters than mother and daughter. "I see a strong family resemblance."

She smiled softly. "My grandmother was very proud that day. She had just been promoted to master weaver."

"Is that difficult to achieve?"

"She studied for ten years, working as an apprentice for minimum wage. She was the first woman to ever achieve such an honor. Until then it had been only men."

Cassie moved to the next photo. "And this material," she said, "was used in the coronation gown of Queen Elizabeth." Like a docent in a museum, she walked him down the wall of pictures, patiently explaining each and every one.

When she was finished, she looked at him and smiled.

"Impressive," he said.

"Now close your eyes."

"What?"

"Close them." She took his hand. He heard a door opening and knew immediately that she had taken him into the heart of the factory. "Smell," she said.

He did as she asked, inhaling a distinct, sweet smell. "I noticed it on my first day here," he said. "What is it?"

"The smell of history. Old machinery and fresh silk."

He opened his eyes. She led him over to an old loom. "See those," she said, pointing to the threads gathered on the loom. "By the end of tomorrow those threads will be part of an intricately patterned piece of fabric."

He nodded toward a machine in the corner. It looked like something one might see in a museum. "What is that?"

"It's a device for twisting cords for tassels. It was invented by Leonardo da Vinci. It hasn't been changed much since."

She took his hand and ran it over the fabric on the loom. "Does this feel familiar?"

Despite the intricate pattern and the number of threads that had been used, the weave was so tight it felt like a single piece of sleek silk. "Should it?" he asked.

"This is the same material that's hanging in your bedroom in your boat. The material you don't even recognize took two people one whole week to make."

"I'll be sure to appreciate it when I get back."

She sighed. "Can you?"

"What do you mean by that?"

She shrugged, not wanting to answer. But she didn't have to.

He knew what she had been implying—perhaps he wasn't capable of recognizing beauty.

But she was wrong, he thought, as he admired her delicate, rosebud lips. He could not only recognize magnificence, he could appreciate it. "Just because I didn't recognize my drapes doesn't mean I don't appreciate them."

"It's not a matter of appreciation. It's a matter of noticing. I think if you had noticed you would have appreciated them. But you were too busy making the money needed to buy such luxuries." She shook her head. "I think a lot of people are like that. Life is something they endure. They're so busy surviving that they don't really live. So busy making money that it somehow loses its value." She looked around her. "That's why I'm so fond of this place. It reminds me of a simpler time. A time when making a living with your hands was nothing to be ashamed of."

"It's still not."

"Everything is equated with money. If it doesn't make money, it's not appreciated."

"That's true in a sense," he admitted. "But, Cassie, you can't stop progress. And you can't turn back the clock."

She hesitated and then nodded sadly. "Unfortunately."

Hunter knew right then and there that Willa was wrong. It was not revenge that motivated Cassie, but love.

It was nearly two in the morning by the time they returned to Cassie's house. Despite the late hour, neither was ready to end the evening. They built a roaring fire and settled next to each other on the couch with steaming mugs of hot chocolate.

Cassie leaned her head against Hunter's shoulder. Once again she was tempted to speak her thoughts out loud and tell him that she wished the night would never end.

But she had learned her lesson before. She would stay quiet, no matter how difficult that might be.

"This is nice," he said, brushing her cheek. "I almost wish I didn't have to leave tomorrow."

"Are you returning to the Bahamas?" she asked as coolly as she could manage.

He shook his head. "Paris."

"Oh," she said, obviously disappointed. "How long will you be gone?"

He hesitated. After a pause he said, "Look, Cassie…"

She knew what was coming next. And she was to blame. There had been desperation in her voice. And now she would get the speech. I never meant to lead you on. I never meant to imply that things were more serious than they seemed. We barely know each other….

And she had no doubt he meant it. But she had seen tenderness in his eyes and felt passion in his arms. She didn't want to think that the feelings he had brought to life inside her would be silenced once more.

But there was no choice. She had no more power over the fate of their relationship than she had over the fate of her beloved mill.

She held a finger to his lips. She couldn't bear to hear it. "Hunter, I didn't mean it to sound the way it did. Let's just enjoy tonight, okay?"

But the mood was ruined. She straightened slightly, pulling away. Hunter cupped her chin and directed her back toward him. "Cassie," he said. "I need to talk to you about the mill."

So she had been right about the speech. But she was wrong about the subject matter.

Had he changed his mind about selling her the mill? Is that why he seemed so distracted? Was he feeling guilty?

"I've decided to give you the patent."

She sat so still, she held her breath. "The patent for Bodyguard?" she said finally.

"That's right."

"But we can only afford our original offer—"

"I don't care about the money."

"You don't?"

He shook his head. "But I do care about you. And I can't sit back and watch you walk into a situation that I know is destined for failure. Which is why I'm going to provide the financial backing for the release of Bodyguard. I've assigned a marketing team to help you with the rollout."

It was better than she could have hoped. She hugged him. "Thank you."

But he did not respond. He pulled back and flashed her a sad smile. "You're still going to need a lot of luck, Cassie."

And suddenly all she could think about was him. She did not want to say goodbye. Not then. Not ever.

He said, "I do, however, have one demand."

There was a catch? "What?"

"Come with me to Paris."

"Paris?" She had dreamed of visiting Paris since she was a child.

"I have some work in a neighboring town, but it won't take me long."

"I don't know what to say."

"Say you'll come." He paused. "It's just a week. One week and you'll be back."

It was not Paris that enticed her so much, but the idea of spending an entire week with Hunter.

"Well?" he asked.

She looked into his kind and gentle eyes. They were not the eyes of a corporate baron. They were the eyes of a man who was willing to listen when others wouldn't. A man who was willing to give her a chance. They were the eyes of the man she loved.

There was no guarantee their relationship would last. Nor was there any guarantee she would not return from Paris with a broken heart. But it didn't seem to matter. "What time do we leave?"

Fourteen

Cassie's skilled fingers flew over the loom. She glanced around her. The floor where people normally worked in quiet or hushed tones was a flurry of activity. It had been a long time since Cassie had seen everyone so happy. It was as if the dark cloud had lifted.

So why wasn't she jumping for joy? After all, she had every reason to be ecstatic. The mill was saved, the patent returned. She had woken up in the arms of the man with whom she was desperately in love. They were leaving that night for Paris.

Luanne leaned forward and said, "When are you returning?"

"In a week."

"Take your time," said Ruby.

"You deserve it," said Luanne.

Cassie attempted to smile. What was wrong with her?

Why did she feel so vulnerable? As if the floor was about to give way underneath her?

Because Hunter had not said the words *I love you?*

Why would he? After all, they had only known each other for a short time.

Unfortunately it was not that simple. She suspected her affection would never be returned.

For, despite his humble origins, Hunter was a man who prized material wealth above all else. He was a product of the society he helped support, the fast-paced corporate world where emotional connections took a second place to business contacts.

Cassie was suddenly aware that the din in the room had silenced.

Suddenly she heard a voice that sent chills down her spine. "Cassie?"

She turned. Willa was standing behind her.

"Can I talk to you for a moment?"

"She's busy," Luanne said.

"It's all right," Cassie said. She smiled affectionately at her friends. She knew they were being protective, but she could handle herself.

She followed Willa into the empty hall.

Willa shut the door behind them and turned to face Cassie. "I'm going to be leaving soon. I wanted to congratulate you before I left."

Cassie couldn't help but think this was some sort of trick. What was Willa up to? "Thank you," she said.

"I hope there are no hard feelings."

"None."

"Excellent," Willa said. She nodded toward the picture behind Cassie. It was a black-and-white close-up of threads gathered in a ponytail on a Jacquard loom. "You took that photo, didn't you?"

Cassie glanced behind her. She had taken the picture while still in high school. Her grandmother had shown it to the manager of the mill, who had insisted on framing it and hanging it on the wall. "Yes," she said.

"You're really quite good. It's a shame you never had a chance to pursue your photography."

"I'm happy working here," Cassie said.

"So you say. Still, it's a shame your talent will never go anywhere. I mean, with your new responsibilities and all. You're hardly going to have time to brush your teeth, much less explore the arts."

"Is there a point to this, Willa? I need to get going."

"That's right," Willa said. "You have a plane to catch, don't you?"

Cassie glared at her.

"I wanted to congratulate you on that, as well. Scoring a trip with Hunter Axon. My, my. Very impressive. An affair with a man like him…well, that's quite a notch in your belt."

"Goodbye, Willa," Cassie said, her hand on the door.

"Of course, that's all it will ever be," Willa said. "An affair."

Had Cassie not been having the same thoughts, she might have been able to keep walking. But because Willa seemed to be reading her mind, because she was saying exactly what, deep down, Cassie had been thinking, she hesitated.

Willa took a step toward her and said, "Do you know why he's going to France?"

"He has business."

"He's buying a wine-making factory. It's in a small village outside of Paris. Families from the town have worked there for generations. We're getting it for quite a steal. See, they don't want to sell, but they have no choice. They're in debt. So Hunter's going to shut it down and produce the label in California."

Cassie was silent.

"All those families that have depended on this factory for hundreds of years are going to be displaced."

Cassie looked away. "Why are you telling me this?"

"I'm pointing out the obvious. I've known Hunter for years."

Cassie had heard all she could bear. She opened the door.

"It will never work," Willa said. "And you know that. You're just postponing the inevitable. And quite frankly, you have too much work to do to be so distracted. From one woman to another, the last thing you need is another heartbreak."

"I said goodbye."

"Oh, before I go… If you do get lonely, you might want to

call Oliver. I've broken it off with him, and the poor dear isn't handling it very well."

"Too bad," Cassie said. "You seemed so well suited for each other." She slipped inside, shutting the door behind her.

As she made her way back to the loom, she was aware that work had stopped and every eye was on her.

"Honey?" Luanne said. "Are you all right?"

No, she wasn't. In one split second her world had spun out of control, her hope for the future dashed.

Hunter was going to France to shut down another plant. To wreak havoc on more lives.

And for what? Money? Didn't he have enough of that?

But what did she think? That he had changed? That her short time with him had made him see the error of his ways?

"Why don't you sit down," Mabel said, touching her arm.

But Cassie barely heard her. How could Hunter do that? It was hard to understand how someone who could be so kind and caring one moment could be so unfeeling the next.

And as much as she cared about Hunter, could she really be with someone who could inflict so much pain on others?

But her question was, in all probability, moot.

Actions Speak Louder Than Words. And Hunter's actions were sending her a message. Nothing had changed. He was still the same man who had threatened their community. The man who worshipped money.

The man who would never love her.

And Willa, as much as she hated to admit it, was right. Cassie was too busy to let herself be distracted by a fling. Even if it came with a mill, a trip to Paris and a marketing plan.

Hunter finished reading the contract. It detailed the transfer of Demion Mills to the workers, emphasizing that his team would help with the marketing of Bodyguard.

It was the first time he had given back a property. Yet he had no regrets. It felt good to be helping the community. To have people thanking him instead of cursing his name.

In fact, he was, for the first time in years, happy.

Was it possible?

It was such a strange feeling for him that he wasn't quite sure how to respond.

Of course, his happiness was due to more than just the mill. The reason for his newfound bliss could be summed up in one word: Cassie.

From the moment he met her he realized this was no ordinary affair. He was entirely bewitched. It was difficult to believe that a woman who could be so enticing, give him the most sexual pleasure he had ever experienced, could also be so innocent.

But his attraction was based on more than just sex. She was the most honest, dedicated and loyal person he had ever met. Seemingly unimpressed by monetary wealth, she valued those things that Hunter had almost forgotten existed, the little everyday occurrences that made life special. Whether to admire a sunset or to feel soft fabric, she encouraged him to slow down, to stop and notice things that he had taken for granted.

His decision to invite Cassie to Paris had been spontaneous yet inevitable. Usually he did not enjoy having women with him on business trips. They were distractions at a time when he preferred to be focused. But Cassie was different. With Cassie, it was the business that was the distraction. He would've preferred to spend all of his time with her. He did not want to be apart from her. Not now or ever.

Hunter was distracted by a knock on the door. He glanced up and smiled as he saw Cassie.

"I was just about to come and see you," he said. "I spoke to the travel agent. She's booked us in an old inn in Loiret. The vineyard I'm buying isn't far away. You'll have a couple of days to sightsee but I'll be back in time for dinner." He stood up and walked over toward her, put his hands around her waist. "After which, I'm going to take you to Paris. I'm going to show you whatever you want to see."

She stepped backward, away from him. She bit her lower lip,

and her eyes, usually bright and full of life, looked glazed with despair.

Alarmed, he asked, "What's wrong?"

She met his gaze directly. "I can't go to Paris."

"Why not?"

"I have responsibilities here, responsibilities that can't wait."

"Cassie," he said patiently. "It's two weeks before the mill is officially transferred. And my marketing team isn't arriving until next week. You'll be back in plenty of time."

She glanced away. "My reason for not going has nothing to do with the mill."

An icy fear cloaked his heart. "What, then?"

"Why didn't you tell me you were going to Paris to take over a company?"

He felt a stab of guilt. But why should he feel guilty? He was not ashamed of what he did. Was he? "I didn't think it would make a difference."

She shook her head. "It's not right. Buying companies and putting people out of work."

"It's not that simple," he said. "I've built three brand-new factories in China employing hundreds of workers, people who were desperate to earn money."

"That's commendable, but it's not as if you're running a non-profit organization. What happens to all those people whose jobs you've taken away?"

"Not everyone lives in Shanville, Cassie. In some situations workers are more than happy to be offered a severance package." He argued mechanically, presenting her with the same defenses he used to ease his guilty conscience. "These are companies close to bankruptcy."

"You're putting people out of work. You're closing up mom-and-pop businesses that have been in families for years. You're making money off other people's misfortunes."

His eyes hardened as he was overcome by a raw and primitive grief. "Is that what you think of me? That I'm some sort of…monster?"

She stood up. "No. That's not the person I see. But…" Her voice faded.

"These businesses," he said, taking a step toward her, "these mom-and-pops that I take over, are destined for failure. I save whatever is left and turn them into profit-making ventures."

"For whom? Not for the families who have given them their life." She shook her head. "I'm sorry, Hunter. But I think it's commendable only if you prize money above all else."

So this was it? She was breaking off their relationship because she did not like his job?

He had the feeling it went deeper than that. And as much as it pained him, he needed to know.

He said, "Don't use my job as an excuse to stay away from me. If you have a problem with me or something I've done, I would hope you try and talk to me about it before you reach a decision."

"Talking about it won't change anything. You are who you are."

You are who you are.

It was personal.

"I see," he managed. "And your mind is made up?"

She nodded and turned to leave.

"Cassie," said Hunter, stopping her. But what could he say? How could he stop her from walking out the door when she was right? He did not deserve her. He never had.

He held up the papers on his desk. "Your contract."

She walked back toward him. As he handed her the contract, their hands touched. Hunter was once again overcome by the desire to say something, anything to change her mind. But what?

Instead she spoke. "I'm very grateful for everything you've done for me."

He let go of her hand. "Good luck, Cassie," he said.

That was it. It was over. It would have happened sooner or later, wouldn't it? So, better to get it out of the way. Better not to wait. She was right, he told himself.

When she glanced up at him, he could see her eyes were filled with tears. She reached around her neck and unclasped the necklace.

"I want you to have this," she said, offering it to him.

"No," he said. "I can't accept that."

"It's not worth anything but it means a lot to me." She put the necklace on the desk. She shook her head and turned away. "I will never forget you," she said softly.

Fifteen

Cassie stood behind her loom as the last of the workers left.

She was alone.

It was getting late and she knew that she should leave, as well. But she was not looking forward to returning home, back to the same place where, just that morning, she and Hunter had made love. She knew the minute she walked in the door she would be overcome by all the emotion she had struggled to hold at bay.

She closed her eyes. Once again she asked herself the question that had haunted her all day: Had she done the right thing?

Or had she just made the biggest mistake of her life?

She knew without a doubt she had passed up the chance of a lifetime. Hunter was unlike any man she had ever met before, any man she would ever meet again.

When she closed her eyes, she could still feel his touch. He had made her feel special. Desired.

She walked to the window and looked up at the stars. Hunter was miles away by now, his plane heading toward France. Did he regret the end of their relationship? Or was he looking forward to a new beginning?

She would never know. She doubted she would ever speak to Hunter again.

Hunter had been sitting in the airport for nearly two hours. Normally he would have been agitated, eager to get to his next destination.

But not tonight. In fact, he welcomed the delay. He was in no rush to leave Shanville.

To leave Cassie.

It had been hours since he last saw her, but it already felt like a lifetime. He had racked his brain trying to think of a solution. According to Cassie, however, the only solution would be for him to give up his company, to devote himself toward a more humanitarian profession.

He pulled out her necklace once again. *It's not worth much...*

How could she say that? It had been her mother's necklace. Cassie wore it every day. He knew how much it meant to her.

He had not felt right accepting such a gift.

He knew he would eventually return it to Cassie. But not yet. He could not bear to part with the only reminder he had of her.

"I just spoke to Jack," Willa said. "We should be leaving momentarily." She sat down next to Hunter and said, "I can't say I'm sorry to be leaving. The sooner I forget about Oliver the better."

"I'm sorry it didn't work out between you two."

She shrugged her shoulders. "I'm not. I guess you could say he lost his appeal."

"Coincidentally at the same time he lost his job."

She smiled. "Oh, well. Win some, lose some."

"You know," he said, "you haven't asked where Cassie is."

"Oh, Cassie. That's right. She was supposed to join you, wasn't she?"

Hunter looked at her, his eyes narrowing. He had suspected that Willa might have had something to do with Cassie's sudden change of heart. Her reaction just confirmed his suspicions.

"Oh, dear," Willa said. She sighed sympathetically. "Are you two having some problems?"

"You might say so," he said calmly.

"Well," she said, shrugging, "it's probably better this way. Cassie belongs here with her own kind."

His face paled with anger. "Own kind?"

Oblivious to his reaction, she smiled again. "You know what I mean. Her own class of people."

"I see," Hunter said, his voice heavy with contempt.

Willa checked her watch. "It's time for me to leave," she said, brushing off her skirt, "perhaps we should go."

"What did you say to her?" His voice was quiet, his tone cold and lashing.

"What?"

"What did you say to Cassie?"

Willa crossed her arms in front of her. "Nothing I wouldn't say to you—respectfully, of course."

"Like?"

"What does it matter?" She shook her head. "I think it was honorable of you to give her the mill, I really do. However, that said, what are you going to have to do to continue to please her? Every time she raises an objection about some poor people being displaced, what will you do? I mean, let's face it, you're not exactly a philanthropist."

No. No, he wasn't. But that didn't mean he couldn't be.

Suddenly he thought about the expressions on the workers' faces when he informed them he would be shutting down their plant. That the only job they had ever known would be gone forever. Sure there were instances when they welcomed the change, but more times than not there were tears, devastation, even hopelessness. He had done his best to ignore it, to push it out of his mind. He had told himself over and over again that he was actually doing them a favor, but who was he kidding?

He thought about his own father. He had grown up hearing stories about how his father had lost his job. Had his father been grateful to the man who had bought the company where he had worked? Hardly. He had lost the only life he had ever known.

How had this happened? Hunter looked down at his hands. When did he turn into one of the very people he'd grown up hating?

"We are who we are, Hunter. And I happen to think you're pretty terrific." Willa put her arm in his. "Shall we go?"

He was repulsed by Willa's touch. He suddenly saw her for who she was: a mean, vindictive, small-minded woman. He shook off her arm and asked her, "What do you think their chances are?"

"Their?"

"Cassie and the rest of the people trying to turn the mill around."

"The marketing team will help, that's for certain. But quite frankly, I think it's still a waste of your money. After all, they're going to have to price themselves out of the market. The wages they pay their workers are so high they'll never be able to make a product that people can actually afford. I don't care how good it is." She shook her head. "They were fools, each and every one of them. And they're about to pay the price."

Once again Hunter felt inside his pocket, desperately clutching the necklace that Cassie gave him.

Suddenly he had an idea. What if he were to provide financial backing until Demion Mills began turning a profit? What if, he thought, his pulse racing, he offered that service to other companies, as well?

Suddenly he felt as if the clouds had cleared. He saw his future as it could be. Instead of buying out the companies struggling for survival, he could use his expertise to turn their fortunes around.

But it would require a huge commitment. It would require walking away from the company he had built from scratch.

Only one thing was clear.

Nothing seemed to matter anymore but Cassie.

He stood. He took his briefcase and started toward the door.

"Hunter," Willa said. "Where are you going? The tarmac is that way."

He walked back toward Willa and stopped. "Do you think the severance package that we offered the Demion Mill workers was fair?"

"Yes, of course. I drew it up myself."

"Good. That's exactly what you'll receive. I'll direct the office to cut you a check. In the meantime, the plane will be happy to take you wherever you might want to go."

Willa stepped away, stunned. "You're firing me?"

"Just like you told the workers at Demion Mills: 'Don't view this as a negative. View it as a chance to start over.'" He nodded. "Goodbye, Willa."

Sixteen

Cassie closed her eyes and took her fingers off the loom, taking a momentary break. It was nearly midnight. Despite her fatigue, she had been unable to bring herself to leave the mill.

"Cassie?"

She opened her eyes. Hunter was standing in the doorway.

Cassie just stared, too astonished to speak.

"Can I talk to you?" he asked.

He looked exhausted. He was still wearing his suit, but his tie was loose, his rumpled shirt open at the neck. His hair was tousled, and he had circles under his eyes. "What are you doing here?" she asked. "I thought you went to France."

"I'm not going."

"What...why?"

He walked toward her. "You were right this afternoon. I am what I am. And my job is such that it doesn't allow for a lot of philanthropy."

"I'm sorry I said that."

"No," he said. "I didn't come here for apologies." He swallowed. "At least, not from you. I wanted to explain to you that my company is not what I had originally intended. I've always liked a challenge. I was attracted to the idea that I could go into businesses that were struggling and fix them. At least, that's what I told myself I was doing. I liked the idea of turning a business around—textiles, steel, wine, it didn't matter. I tried to ignore the fact that people were losing their jobs, that whole economies were ruined. I told myself that the businesses were struggling and if I didn't take them over, those people would lose their jobs anyway."

"That's probably true."

"But that doesn't make what I do right. And it doesn't excuse what I did, either."

She stared at him, her heart pounding. "What are you saying?"

"I'm saying I think it's time for a career change."

"A career change?"

"Instead of specializing in takeovers, I'm thinking that perhaps I should reconsider. Turn my energy toward helping those struggling companies survive."

Was she hearing him correctly? "Just like you're helping Demion Mills?"

"That's right."

He stopped at the loom. He ran his fingers over the threads she had just woven.

"That's what you came back to tell me?" she asked quietly.

He took another step toward her. He was standing so close their lips were practically touching. "That's not all," he said. His eyes blazed and glowed as he took her hands in his. "I've fallen in love with you."

He had fallen in love.

He loved her.

Cassie closed her eyes as the shock of his words hit her full force.

"If you give me a chance, I'm willing to try and be a better man."

She was certain she was dreaming. She had fallen asleep at her loom and would wake up alone in a cold, dark, empty room.

"Give me an opportunity to prove that I'm worthy of your love."

She opened her eyes and stared at him, unable to speak. He let go of her hands and pulled her necklace out of his pocket.

His fingers brushed her nape as he fastened it around her neck. "Do I have a chance?" he whispered in her ear.

She twisted around to face him. She once again remembered what her grandmother said. *Actions Speak Louder Than Words.* And with that, she kissed him.

Epilogue

It was the opening of the Shanville Gallery, a nonprofit center that featured the work of local artists. And from the crowd that had gathered in the small, renovated building in the center of town, it was a success.

Thanks to her husband's connections, the gathering included local and not-so-local stars. The governor of New York was there along with various politicians and personalities. All had turned out to show their support for Shanville, which was becoming known as a mecca for the arts.

But like Shanville itself, there was no pretension here. All the invitees were dressed casually, supping on a buffet that included dishes the local diner was famous for: meat loaf and macaroni and cheese.

Cassie spotted her husband across the room. They had been married for three years, but the sight of him still caused her heart to skip a beat. He stood in the doorway, a grin spreading across his lips as their eyes met.

Their wedding had been a fairy-tale ending to a not-so-traditional courtship—an affair that she felt certain would have restored her grandmother's pride and her belief in the power of sex.

Afterward, Hunter moved into Cassie's home, and together he and his new bride launched a foundation specifically designed to help family businesses in need.

In the three years that had passed since their wedding, Hunter had become a vital part of Shanville and Demion Mills. He seemed to have no problem leaving his corporate image and expensive toys behind, easily adapting to the down-to-earth lifestyle of small-town living.

It was a change, he claimed, that he had been anticipating a long time. All he needed was the right woman to make it all come true.

They walked toward each other, drawn together like magnets. He took her in his arms and kissed her on the lips. "I'm so proud of you," he said.

"Why?"

"You worked hard for this opening."

"We," she said. "We worked hard."

For the past few months Cassie and Hunter had met at the gallery after work, doing much of the refurbishing themselves. Hunter had long ago proven himself surprisingly adept with a hammer and nails. Some of Cassie's friends had been amazed that a man worth millions was willing to perform physical labor. But not Cassie. Hunter enjoyed working with his hands. He had become an excellent craftsman, capable of replicating the intricate wood carvings that were found on so many old homes.

"Cassie?"

Cassie turned. Her old friend Luanne was there behind her. "You have some visitors." She pointed to the door.

Willa and Oliver stood side by side.

"What are they doing here?" Ruby whispered, hurrying over.

But Cassie was not surprised to see them. After all, they had been invited.

Soon after she and Hunter married, Hunter had encouraged her to renew her friendship with Oliver. He had been her oldest and dearest friend, Hunter had argued. It was a relationship worth preserving. She took her husband's advice and she and Oliver redefined their relationship as two old friends. Oliver soon confided that he had never recovered from the demise of his relationship with Willa. Cassie counseled him to reconcile, and one morning Oliver announced that not only had he and Willa reconciled, they had married.

Unfortunately for Oliver, however, it soon became clear that being the mistress of the "Demion estate" did not seem to satisfy Willa. Opinionated and haughty, Willa was every bit as abrasive as she had been at the mill. Still, Willa had become such a colorful personality in Shanville that it was hard to imagine the town without her. But most of the town residents were still cool to her, never having forgiven her for her previous offenses.

They seemed to delight in knocking Willa off her throne. And this, apparently, was another one of those times.

Cassie shook her head. Both Willa and Oliver were dressed in formal attire, as if attending a ball. Willa looked resplendent in a draping red dress. Oliver was wearing a white tuxedo.

Cassie saw Willa's eyes open wide in horror as she looked at the casually dressed guests. She gave Oliver a nasty look and swatted him across the stomach.

Cassie heard Luanne snicker. She looked at her friend suspiciously. "Luanne, is there a reason they might have thought this event was formal?"

Luanne shrugged and averted her gaze. "Maybe."

Cassie rolled her eyes. Hunter tried to hide his smile by pretending to cough.

She and Hunter went over to welcome their guests. Afterward, as they watched Willa and Oliver head toward the buffet, Hunter said, "You really are amazing. Only you could've made them feel so comfortable. That was very gracious of you."

She smiled and said, "I have every reason to be gracious. After all, as of today, all my wishes have come true."

He glanced at her. "Revenge on Willa?"

"No," she said, laughing.

"Let me guess," he said. "Saving Demion Mills was wish number one…."

"No," she said. "You were number one. Demion Mills was number two."

"And the art gallery was number three?"

"I wanted the gallery, but it wasn't a wish."

"Willa and Oliver come dressed to serve?"

She laughed and said, "Nope."

"You've been promoted to master weaver?"

"Not yet," she said.

Suddenly his eyes opened wide as she touched her stomach. He smiled.

Wish number three. They were soon to be family.

With a holler, Hunter picked her up and spun her around.

"But," she said, "I do have a single demand."

"Anything," he said. "As you know I've never been able to resist you."

"Just love me."

"That's a request I'll never deny," he said, settling the deal with a kiss.

* * * * *

Silhouette® Desire®

**Coming in March 2005
from Silhouette Desire**

The next installment in

DYNASTIES: THE ASHTONS

SOCIETY-PAGE SEDUCTION
by Maureen Child
(SD #1639)

When dashingly handsome billionaire
Simon Pearce was deserted at the altar,
wedding planner Megan Ashton filled in for the
bride. Before long, their faux romance turned into
scorching passion. Yet little did Simon know Megan
had not only sparked excitement between his
sheets, she'd also brought scandal to his door....

Available at your favorite retail outlet.

An Invitation for Love

hot tips

Find a special way to invite your guy into your Harlequin Moment. Letting him know you're looking for a little romance will help put his mind on the same page as yours. In fact, if you do it right, he won't be able to stop thinking about you until he sees you again!

Send him a long-stemmed rose tied to an invitation that leaves a lot up to the imagination.

Autograph a favorite photo of you and tape it on the appointed day in his day planner. Block out the hours he'll be spending with you.

Send him a local map and put an *X* on the place you want him to meet you. Write: "I'm lost without you. Come find me. Tonight at 8." Use magazine cutouts and photographs to paste images of romance and the two of you all over the map.

Send him something personal that he'll recognize as yours to his office. Write: "If found, please return. Owner offers reward to anyone returning item by 7:30 on Saturday night." Don't sign the card.

Are you a chocolate lover?

Try WALDORF CHOCOLATE FONDUE—
a true chocolate decadence

While many couples choose to dine out on Valentine's Day, one of the most romantic things you can do for your sweetheart is to prepare an elegant meal—right in the comfort of your own home.

Harlequin asked John Doherty, executive chef at the Waldorf-Astoria Hotel in New York City, for his recipe for seduction—the famous Waldorf Chocolate Fondue....

WALDORF CHOCOLATE FONDUE
Serves 6-8

2 cups water
½ cup corn syrup
1 cup sugar
8 oz dark bitter chocolate, chopped
1 pound cake (can be purchased in supermarket)
2–3 cups assorted berries
2 cups pineapple
½ cup peanut brittle

Bring water, corn syrup and sugar to a boil in a medium-size pot. Turn off the heat and add the chopped chocolate. Strain and pour into fondue pot. Cut cake and fruit into cubes and 1-inch pieces. Place fondue pot in the center of a serving plate, arrange cake, fruit and peanut brittle around pot. Serve with forks.

Looking for a seductive cocktail?

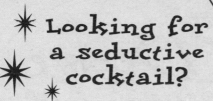

Try *Ero-Desiac*— a dazzling martini

With its warm apricot walls yet cool atmosphere, Verlaine is quickly becoming one of New York's hottest nightspots. Verlaine created a light, subtle yet seductive martini for Harlequin: the Ero-Desiac. Sake warms the heart and soul, while jasmine and passion fruit ignite the senses....

The Ero-Desiac

Combine vodka, sake, passion fruit puree and jasmine tea. Mix and shake. Strain into a martini glass, then rest pomegranate syrup on the edge of the martini glass and drizzle the syrup down the inside of the glass.

COMING NEXT MONTH

#1639 SOCIETY-PAGE SEDUCTION—Maureen Child
Dynasties: The Ashtons
When dashingly handsome billionaire Simon Pearce was deserted at the altar, wedding planner Megan Ashton filled in for the bride. Before long, their faux romance turned into scorching passion. Yet little did Simon know Megan had not only sparked excitement between his sheets, she'd also brought scandal to his door….

#1640 A MAN APART—Joan Hohl
The moment rancher Justin Grainger laid eyes on sexy Hannah Deturk, he vowed not to leave town without getting into her bed. Their whirlwind affair left them both wanting more. But Hannah feared falling for a loner like Justin could only mean heartache…unless she convinced him to be a man apart no longer.

#1641 HER *FIFTH* HUSBAND?—Dixie Browning
Divas Who Dish
She had a gift for picking the wrong men…her four failed marriages were a testament to her lousy judgment. So when interior designer Sasha Lasiter met stunningly sexy John Batchelor Smith she fervently fought their mutual attraction. But John was convinced Sasha's fifth time would be the charm— only if he was the groom!

#1642 TOTAL PACKAGE—Cait London
Heartbreakers
After being dumped by her longtime love, photographer Sidney Blakely met the total package in smart, and devastatingly handsome Danya Stepanov. Before long he had Sidney spoiled rotten, but she couldn't help wondering whether this red-hot relationship could survive her demanding career.

#1643 UNDER THE TYCOON'S PROTECTION—Anna DePalo
Her life was in danger, but the last person proud Allison Whittaker wanted to protect her was her old crush, bodyguard Connor Rafferty. Having been betrayed by Connor before, Allison still burned with anger, but close quarters rekindled the fiery desire that raged between them…and ignited deeper emotions that put her heart in double jeopardy.

#1644 HIGH-STAKES PASSION—Juliet Burns
Ever since his career-ending injury, ex-rodeo champion Mark Malone walked around with a chip on his shoulder. Housekeeper Aubrey Tyson arranged a high-stakes game of poker to lighten this sexy cowboy's mood— but depending on the luck of the draw, she could wind up in his bed…!